Mabel

Rescue Me Mail-Order Brides

Cheryl Wright

Mabel

(Rescue Me Mail-Order Brides)

*Note: Mabel is part of a multi-author series

Copyright ©2023 by Cheryl Wright

Cover Artist: Nancy Fraser

Editing: Sarah Lamb

Dedication

To Margaret Tanner, my very dear friend and fellow author, for her enduring encouragement and friendship.

To Alan, my husband of over forty-eight years, who has been a relentless supporter of my writing and dreams for many years.

To You, my wonderful readers, who encourage me to continue writing these stories. It is such a joy knowing so many of you enjoy reading my stories as much as I love writing them for you.

Table of Contents

Chapter One

Hell's Gate, Montana – 1880s

Breathless, Mabel McArthur crouched down behind the boxes in the livery. She hoped and prayed no one saw her run in there.

"Mabel! Mabel, my darling, where are you?" Vern's voice came through loud and clear. Mabel shuddered as he came dangerously close and crouched down even further. Despite the chill of the day, sweat poured down her face. "Mabel?" This time, his voice was far more gentle. He spoke as though he were caressing her cheek.

As Vern's fiancée, Mabel was protected from all the terrible things that happened in town. The shootings, the bashings, and the killings. He ensured she wasn't harmed and made certain she had everything she would ever need.

Vern often told Mabel he loved her, but kept her locked away unless she was with him. It was for her own safety, he said when she questioned him. According to Vern, there were far too many bad things going on in town. Whenever she suggested they move elsewhere, he refused. Now Mabel knew why.

They were to marry next month, and while at first it seemed an exciting prospect, things had soured between them. Everything changed when Mabel snuck out of her room at the boarding house where Vern *kept her safe*.

Breakfast was brought to her room each morning, and after she'd eaten, Mabel would have a long, leisurely bath. Later, Vern would collect her and they'd go for a stroll around town. Occasionally, they would go for a drive through the hillside, depending on the weather.

She was weary of doing the same things day after day, night after night. Tonight, she'd taken matters into her own hands and left the boarding house. Mabel had begun to feel suspicious about her fiancée's motives, hence her reason for leaving that day. She ran to the hotel, where she was certain she would find Vern.

And that's where she saw it.

Vern stood over a young cowboy. He was battered and bleeding. Mabel had seen him on their strolls around town. Vern had a gun in his hand. Mabel's heart thudded as she watched in horror. Vern grinned, then put the gun to the other man's head and pulled the trigger. The cowboy lay lifeless on the ground as Vern stood over him, laughing.

That was when he noticed her standing nearby.

Mabel shoved a fist in her mouth to stop herself from screaming, then ran as though her life depended on it.

She was convinced it did.

The constant movement of the train had Mabel nodding off. "No!" she shouted, not meaning to be so vocal. It was dangerous to sleep in such a public place. What if Vern had followed her? He could be on this very train.

Mabel shivered. The mere thought sent daggers of terror down her spine. After witnessing the death of that cowboy, she wouldn't put anything past her fiancée.

Guilt filled her. Little had Mabel known Vern's riches came from killing those who opposed him. Or defeated him at cards. Or goodness knew what else.

Tears threatened to break through, but that was the last thing Mabel wanted right now. She was in public, on a train, and couldn't afford to have the focus on her. What if one of Vern's cronies had followed her?

Reading a discarded newspaper, Mabel had spotted an advertisement for mail-order brides. Until then, she'd been riding the trains with no goal in mind. She switched her destination at various stations, ensuring she left no sign of where she was or where she'd been. When she alighted at Little Bridge, where the bridal agency was located, she was delighted to discover her luck was about to change.

Without realizing it, Raymond Carpenter was about to become her savior. According to Myrtle Cunningham, the agency owner, her soon-to-be husband was a rancher. That suited Mabel just fine.

From the little she understood, most ranches were in the middle of nowhere. That was exactly what she needed—total and utter isolation. A place where no one knew she even existed. By then, she would have a new name, which meant a new identity. It was a pity she couldn't change her hair color. That would really put Vern off her trail. Still, it was too late now. If only she'd thought of it before.

The train slowed. "Now arriving in Pleasant Valley," the conductor called. "Pleasant Valley," he repeated.

This was Mabel's stop. Her heart pounded. What would he be like, her groom? There were no photos, and no description. All she knew was he owned a ranch outside the town of Pleasant Valley. The name alone almost decided for her, but it was the location of her new home that clinched the deal.

Mabel stood as the train slowed, and was thrown to the floor. She heard the scuffle of feet, and the next thing she knew, the conductor was helping her up. "I'm so sorry, Miss. Trains are rather jolting at times." He handed Mabel her coat after dusting it off. It had landed on the floor when she fell. "Are you alright, Miss?" he asked, concern etched on his face.

Still feeling somewhat shocked, Mabel stared at him. She shook her head, trying to clear the fog. "Perhaps you should sit a moment or two, Miss. I won't let the train go until you are ready."

She finally came to her senses. "I'm fine," she said, straightening her back. "My fiancée will wonder where I am." She smiled tentatively and stood.

The conductor reached up and handed Mabel her reticule. That was the full extent of her luggage. Ensuring she left before Vern could find her meant she had no time to pack any of her belongings. Mabel couldn't risk going back to the boarding house. What if Vern had followed her there? Would she also be dead now?

The thought had her heart pounding again. All this time, she believed Vern loved her. Now she wasn't so sure. He had killed that cowboy without a second thought. It made sense he would do the same to her.

"If you're certain, Miss?" the conductor said again. "I'll help you down the step. Can't risk having you fall again." He seemed far more worried about her well-being than Mabel was. She certainly couldn't fault him for that. He led her to the exit and demanded she stay where she was until he was in place to assist her down. "There you go, Miss," he said. "Enjoy your stay."

"Thank you," Mabel said as she glanced about. Which one of these gents was her groom? There were a handful of men on the platform, but it was impossible to guess which one was here to collect her.

Two were quite elderly, and she prayed neither was her husband-to-be. Another rather rotund man hurried toward the train, and Mabel breathed a sigh of relief when he climbed up the steps onto the train. He had only moments to spare before the train departed.

No other men remained, and Mabel panicked. Had she been stood up? Was she about to find out Raymond Carpenter had changed his mind? If that was the case, she did not know what she would do. Vern gave her no money, but paid for whatever she wanted. All she possessed was a handful of coins her father had given her some years ago. It had literally saved her life.

Mabel sat on the hard wooden bench for what seemed forever, but was closer to an hour. The platform was empty of everyone except the conductor and porters. And of course, Mabel.

She dug deep into her reticule and pulled out the letter Myrtle Cunningham had handed her. She read over the letter carefully. Mabel wasn't mistaken—Raymond Carpenter was due to collect her precisely one hour ago.

Myrtle had promised to send a telegram to her groom-to-be, and advise him of her arrival details. Mabel had no doubt she'd done what she promised. She'd provided Mabel with a small allowance for meals and fares, all from her soon-to-be husband.

From his letter to Myrtle, Mabel understood he was an upstanding citizen, a rancher of good standing. A recommendation from the local preacher and the town sheriff had verified the information. It cemented Mabel's decision to marry the man.

"Is everything alright, Miss?" A conductor came out of nowhere and startled Mabel. As a result, she lost her grip on the letter she was holding and it fell to the ground. He leaned down and picked it up. His eyes briefly studied the words, seeming to land on her groom's name. For a moment, he appeared startled. In the next moment, he was completely composed again. It made Mabel wonder if Raymond Carpenter was not the upstanding man he'd been made out to be.

"Do you know a Raymond Carpenter?" she asked the conductor. A porter walking past turned and stared at her with pity. It was clear to Mabel she was being shielded, but from what, she wasn't sure.

The conductor cleared his throat. "I do," he said, then glanced at his hands. Now Mabel was scared. Surely she hadn't gone from one criminal to another?

She took a deep breath and let it out slowly. "Tell me," she said, bracing herself for the worst.

He shook his head. "Not my place," he said gravely. "I will take you to the sheriff's office," he said firmly. "He has far more information than I do."

His words seemed to confirm her biggest fear—she had come all this way to marry a man who was every bit as evil as Vern, her former fiancée. The man she was running from.

If she hadn't already been sitting, Mabel was certain she would have collapsed on the hard wooden bench. Her heart pounded so hard she felt faint.

The empty platform suddenly seemed to echo around her. "Miss? Miss?" Mabel felt herself being laid across the bench. "Call the doc," she heard him say, but the words seemed far away. She'd been through so much lately, and this new information had cemented the fact she was destined to a life made up of dreadful men. She seemed to jump from one murderer to another. Although it hadn't yet been confirmed Raymond Carpenter was a murderer, it seemed a foregone conclusion. At least in Mabel's mind.

"Who did he kill?" she mumbled. In her shocked state, Mabel wasn't even certain she'd said the words out loud.

"The doc will be here shortly," the now familiar voice assured her. Only right now, nothing anyone said could assure her.

She was doomed. Destined for a life of one tragedy after another.

Mabel tried to sit up, but someone held her down. The conductor perhaps?

"It's alright, Miss. Stay there. At least for now." The voice was unfamiliar to Mabel, but it was gentle, soothing even. Warm fingers held her wrist, and she stiffened. "I'm checking your pulse," he said. "Oh, I'm sorry—I'm the local doctor," he added.

Mabel relaxed a little. At least she wasn't being manhandled by just anyone.

"Your heart is racing," he said. "I want you to take a deep breath and let it out slowly." He continued to hold her wrist. "And again."

For some reason, she felt compelled to do whatever he suggested.

It seemed like forever before he spoke again. "I think it's safe for you to sit up now," he said quietly, his fingers still on her wrist. "Slowly," he said, then she felt his hands move to support her.

Mabel still felt unsteady and appreciated his hands holding her upright.

"Open your eyes." His words were firm but not unkind.

Instead, she licked her lips. They seemed drier than she remembered. "I need you to open your eyes," he said again. "I promise you'll come to no harm."

Mabel had no way of confirming what he said was true, but had to trust the man. He was a doctor, after all. That meant he'd taken an oath to cause no harm.

She blinked a couple of times, then opened her eyes. It took a few moments for them to adjust to the light. Then she found herself staring into a pair of striking blue eyes surrounded by gold-framed spectacles. A smile slowly spread across his features, and it put Mable more at ease.

"Welcome back," he said, continuing to grip her. "How do you feel?"

"A little lightheaded, but better than before."

He frowned. "You appeared to be in a state of shock. Is that an accurate assessment?"

Mabel licked her lips and raised her eyebrows in astonishment. "Yes, that's a fair assessment. I've discovered my betrothed is a murderer."

The doctor reeled backwards. "That would be a shock," he said as he composed himself. "I suggest you come to my surgery, where I can monitor you for a while."

Her mind was in turmoil. What would she do now? Mabel obviously couldn't marry a criminal. What were the odds of fleeing one murderer only to end up with another? It had to be unheard of. It was pure bad luck for this to happen to one woman.

"I've got nowhere to go," she whispered. "I'm not sure what I'll do now." Her voice was barely above a whisper. Not that she would tell the doctor, but her funds were critically low. This was not meant to happen. Perhaps she could arrange to become a mail-order bride again, only this time there needed to be a more thorough checking.

"That's settled then. Try to stand." She didn't move, and he frowned. "I'm right here. I won't let you fall."

There really was no choice but to trust his word. Mabel stared into his face, then nodded. She slowly stood; his hands close to her arms. The doc was true to his word and was right there with her every move. "How do you feel now?"

She smiled tentatively. "A little unsteady, but not too bad."

He sat her down slowly. "Let's get you some water," he said, nodding at the conductor. It arrived post-haste, and Mabel sipped it as the doctor had instructed.

After a time of sitting, he had Mabel stand again. This time she was more steady on her feet. "Let's go to my surgery," he said. "It's not far. I'll be by your side, so you'll be fine."

Mabel trusted this man—he made her feel at ease, which was no mean feat. She nodded and they were soon on their way. She appreciated him not commenting on the fact she had no luggage.

"Not much further," he said soon after they'd left the train station. They turned the corner and a large building stood in front of them. The doctor guided her toward the entrance. Mabel studied the brass plate attached to the building.

She stood in stunned silence. "Is this you?" she finally asked, pointing at the plate that showed the doctor's details.

"It certainly is," he said proudly.

"Doctor Earl Carpenter," she read from the brass plate. "Are you related to Raymond Carpenter?"

He frowned. "Raymond is my brother. How did you...? Wait—it was Raymond you came here to marry?" He seemed more confused than ever. "We should go inside. You're still a little unsteady." He stared at her. What was going through his mind? It seemed Earl Carpenter was far removed from his criminal brother.

Chapter Two

Earl studied Mabel as she sat nervously in his sitting room.

Mrs. Halliwell, his housekeeper, had served hot drinks and cake. Mabel ate hungrily. It made him wonder how long it had been since she'd eaten a decent meal.

"That was good," she said as she wiped her lips with the linen napkin.

He smiled. For some strange reason, he felt an affinity with this young woman, flighty as she seemed. "Mrs. Halliwell is an excellent cook," he said, meaning every word. If the housekeeper ever decided to retire, he wasn't sure what he would do. "Now," he said, placing his empty mug on the side table. "Let's talk about you." Mabel wriggled uncomfortably in her chair. "There's not much to tell," she said as she stared into her hands. "Raymond was going to marry me. But I guess if he's in jail…"

"Jail?" Earl was confused. Why on earth did she think his brother was in jail? Mabel appeared more than a little confused by his words.

"He's not in jail? I just thought… well, since he's a criminal…" She glanced across at him and seemed to flounder. "He wasn't a criminal?" Perhaps his confused expression gave him away.

Earl reached across and held her hand. "I don't know how to say this, so I'll just say it—Raymond is dead." She gasped and stiffened at his words. "He wasn't a criminal. Far from it. He was a good man, an honest man. He would have been the best husband."

Emotion threatened to overtake him, and Earl took a moment to compose himself.

"I'm sorry," Mabel whispered. "I'm especially sorry I misunderstood your brother from the little I was told when I arrived here." She squeezed his hand, and Earl realized she was trying to comfort him. "Do you mind me asking what happened?"

Earl glanced up and noticed the tears dancing in her eyes. He wasn't sure if they were for herself, for him, or even for Raymond. He let go of her hand and instantly regretted it. Until that moment, he hadn't realized how much comfort it gave him.

"He was killed by cattle rustlers," Earl said, his voice breaking. His loss was still quite raw.

Mabel seemed quite confused then. "I only found out a few days ago we were to marry."

"He died two days ago," Earl said. His heart pounded at the memory of the sheriff's visit. It was Earl's job to declare his brother's death. It was the hardest thing he'd had to do in his life.

Now he had to decide what to do with his brother's bride. He hated to do it, but he'd have to put her up somewhere in town. Propriety meant she couldn't stay here, even under the circumstances. "You can't stay here," he blurted out without thinking.

"I... I didn't expect to," Mabel said, sounding hurt. She opened her reticule, checking her funds.

"I'll pay," he said. "It is not your fault you've come here unnecessarily." He truly meant it.

She closed her eyes tightly for a long moment before opening them again. "There really was no choice," she told him. "It was the only way to stay alive."

Earl stared at her, not sure how to respond. Then he decided it was a joke, only she wasn't laughing. Instead, tears flowed down her face. He hurried to her side, then kneeled in front of her and offered her his handkerchief, which she accepted. "Should I get the sheriff?" Earl asked, not sure if he was being helpful.

She shook her head but seemed uncertain. Mrs. Halliwell entered the room to remove their soiled dishes and sent him a stern look. What did she think he'd done? If it wasn't so serious, it would be laughable.

"I will arrange accommodation. You stay here. Relax and take it easy." He stood then, realizing how stupid his words were, given everything she'd been through lately.

Mabel nodded, and Earl hurried away. He could fix things for now, but what would happen in a few days' time? Mabel's life was clearly in danger. His brother would have taken good care of her. Did that mean he should do the same?

Her room arranged, Earl strode back home. He checked his watch—less than an hour before patients began streaming through the door. Earl sighed. He really wanted to spend more time with Mabel, wanted to sort everything out for her. Since that was not possible, he would continue with his usual schedule. His patients, especially his elderly patients, would be none too pleased if he canceled.

Earl's head hurt. He knew exactly the reason why— it was Mabel. Not that she was a problem. Not at all. It was her situation that bothered him. His brother had promised her marriage. Mabel believed she would be safe by coming here to Pleasant Valley. He couldn't keep her couped up in the women's boarding house forever.

Well, theoretically, he could. But that wouldn't be fair to Mabel, and Raymond would be appalled that his brother was doing such a thing to the woman he'd promised to marry. Did Raymond know about her situation? Since Mabel had told him the arrangement was made only days ago, he guessed that was a no. Despite that, Earl felt responsible for her.

She was nice enough. A little withdrawn and very skittish. Not that he could blame her, given her dire position. As he reached the door to his home, Earl straightened his back and rolled his shoulders. A decision needed to be made, and he needed to do so soon. The worst thing he could do for Mabel was leave her uncertain of her situation.

It was very obvious she couldn't return to her hometown. If she was forced to leave here, where would she go? It also seemed quite apparent her funds were low. He didn't want to think about the consequences to her well-being if he turned her away.

Earl swallowed as his fingers surrounded the door knob. His heart pounded like it had never done before. He was a doctor, and was used to difficult, and even crisis, situations. This was a quandary he'd never been in before, and it was beginning to stress him.

He vowed to make a decision by the time he reached the sitting room. Whether it was the right one remained to be seen.

Closing the door behind him, Earl braced himself, then headed to the sitting room, where he found Mabel sipping tea and chatting with Mrs. Halliwell. "Oh, you're back, Doctor," his housekeeper said almost accusingly. "Mabel and I have been having a nice little chat." She stood then and studied him closely. "I'll leave you to it." She smiled at Mabel, and rubbed her hand across Mabel's back, then quickly left the room. It was almost as though the woman was sending him a message to do right by Mabel.

He knew what he needed to do, and certainly didn't need to be told. Or guilted into doing it. Earl sat down opposite Raymond's betrothed. "I've arranged a room at the women's boarding house. There's no time limit, so you can stay as long as necessary." His words came out matter-of-fact, which wasn't what he'd intended. "You're going to need supplies—clothes and such," he said, meaning unmentionables. Being the gentleman he was, Earl wouldn't say that to a lady. "I'll ask Mrs. Halliwell to take you to the mercantile. She'll know what you'll need."

She opened her mouth to speak, dismay written all over her face. "I…"

He cut her off before she became distressed. "Don't worry about the cost. I'll pay for whatever you need. Raymond would have done the same." She nodded, but still appeared upset. It was out of his control for now—his patients wouldn't wait.

He stood, and Mabel studied him. "Thank you," she said so quietly he barely heard the words. "I appreciate everything you're doing for me." She shuffled in her chair, clearly uneasy about the position she found herself in. "One day I'll repay your kindness." She turned her head away as tears swam in her eyes.

Earl couldn't even begin to imagine what she was going through. Oh, he thought he did, but it was crystal clear that he had not even an inkling. Despite her protests, he would have a quiet word with the sheriff. He would know what to do. The most important thing right now was to keep Mabel safe and out of harm's way.

Without another word, Earl hurried to the kitchen to find the housekeeper. She turned to look at him. "Well," she said sternly, "what are you doing about that dear girl?" Earl swallowed. Mrs. Halliwell did not mince words. Nor did she let him get away with nonsense. It was then he was struck with reasoning. This was nonsense he was going on with. He had to take control and ensure Mabel's safety. Not think about it, not mull it over, but actually do something to help the dear woman. Had it not been for a terrible tragedy, she would be married to his brother. Mabel would be his sister-in-law and part of his family.

It was clear to him now. All he needed was to work out the details. He turned to the housekeeper. "Would you mind taking Mabel to the mercantile and get whatever she needs—clothes, shoes, unmen... er, you know." He felt his face color and turned away.

"Are we looking for regular clothes, or clothes suitable for the doctor's wife?" She pierced him with her eyes, and Earl felt like crawling into a hole. What was he supposed to say to that? Earl cleared his throat. "I wasn't thinking along those lines." It wasn't true. He had been mulling it over in his mind on the way back from arranging Mabel's accommodation.

Mrs. Halliwell studied him again. "You need to do the right thing by that slip of a girl. Look at her—she's fearful for her life." She reached out and stabbed his chest with her finger. "We both know what your brother would want." This time she almost blinded him with the way she pinned him down with only a look.

Earl threw his hands up in the air, then stared at his shoes.

He was happy with the way things were. Answerable to no one, living life the way he wanted. Worrying only about his patients. It suited him fine. Raymond, on the other hand, yearned for a wife. He'd told Earl he was lonely out there alone on the ranch. Sure, he had men working for him, but it wasn't the same thing.

Thankfully, Raymond's foreman had agreed to take over the ranch temporarily. Earl did not know what he should do about it in the long-term, but he had far more important things to worry about in the meantime. Mabel. She was his biggest concern right now.

He slowly lifted his head. "You're right," Earl said, glancing at his loyal housekeeper. She always seemed to know what was best. "Mabel needs to be cared for. Raymond made a promise to her, and I need to ensure her safety."

The expression on Mrs. Halliwell's face was fierce. "Of course she needs to feel safe, but that girl needs love!" She grimaced at him and went back to what she was doing—washing dishes. She slammed the dishes down in her anger and broke one of the plates.

Earl was taken aback. In all the years Mrs. Halliwell had worked for him, she'd never broken a single thing. Never. Nor had she been so angry with him. Earl knew he deserved the treatment she'd dished out. He was acting like an arrogant fool. There was no reason for him not to marry Mabel. Except perhaps he didn't love her. "You're right, of course," he mumbled. "As always, I'm an arrogant fool. Raymond would not be pleased if I didn't take care of her." His heart rate sped up, and Earl was tempted to check his pulse, but knew the housekeeper would only mock him. "Buy the clothes for a doctor's wife."

He went to turn away and return to the sitting room, but was called back. "Don't you think you should discuss it with Mabel before deciding on her behalf?" She raised her eyebrows at him and pierced him with her frightening stare again. It bothered him the way he could be so easily manipulated by this woman, but she was more than capable of knowing what was best for Mabel. It might not be best for him, but that didn't seem to be a consideration.

"You're right," he mumbled, and headed out of the kitchen. How Mabel would feel about all of this, he had no idea. One thing he was certain about, Raymond would be nodding his approval from above. Knowing his bride-to-be was safe and being cared for would mean a lot to him. And right now, that's all that mattered.

Chapter Three

Mabel stared at Earl, her heart pounding so much she felt faint again. "What do you mean, marry you? I didn't come here to marry you. Raymond was to be my husband." She was truly perplexed. Earl didn't seem particularly pleased about marrying her. In fact, he seemed almost... pressured. She mentally shook herself. That couldn't be right. Surely he wouldn't propose if he didn't mean it?

"It seems the most appropriate thing to do, given the circumstances."

Obviously, love didn't come into the equation since they'd only met hours earlier. Which meant he was either being forced into it, which also didn't seem feasible, or he felt obligated. None of which pleased her. "No," she said firmly. "I don't want to marry you." He reeled back in his chair, clearly shocked. "It is very clear you don't want to marry me, so I won't. Where is my accommodation? I'd like to leave now."

Earl sat there, staring at her. Her answer clearly shocked him. To be honest, she was shocked. He was giving her a safe haven, and she refused. It was a stupid thing to do, but the last thing Mabel wanted was for Earl to feel beholden to her. That wasn't fair. She was a complete stranger and had been foisted on him. She did need to leave as soon as she possibly could. That part was very apparent. She had no intention of putting Earl or Mrs. Halliwell in danger, and that was exactly what she would do if she stayed.

In the back of her mind, Mabel was certain Vern would come looking for her. Despite saying he loved her, Vern wasn't the sort of person to let things lie. Especially knowing she'd watched him kill a man in cold blood. Tears filled her eyes with the memory of the horror she'd witnessed. She turned her head, trying to hide her distress. It apparently didn't work because Earl grimaced, then handed her his handkerchief.

"It's not far. I'll take you there now, if that's what you want. Mrs. Halliwell has agreed to take you to the mercantile and help you choose some clothes."

Anger built up inside her. Why was he doing this? Mabel did not want Earl to feel responsibility toward her. Had she known of Raymond's demise, she would never have come to Pleasant Valley. She wasn't sure what she would have done, but Mabel was certain she would have found another place where she could hide away.

"I don't need..." But she did. Her only possessions were the clothes on her back and her reticule. It had been far too risky to go back home and collect her belongings. Vern would have found her, and she would be dead instead of sitting here in Earl's cozy sitting room.

Earl sat quietly, not saying a word. It was clear by his expression he was both annoyed and confused. "Why don't you go with Mrs. Halliwell, and we can talk some more later?" His manner of speech was one a doctor would use when consoling a patient. In fact, it was the voice he'd used on her only hours ago back at the train station. Was it all an act? She was confused beyond comprehension, and had no idea what to do.

She nodded and felt relief as the housekeeper entered the sitting room. Donning her hat, gloves, and coat, it was clear the woman was ready for their expedition to the mercantile. Mabel stood, and the room spun.

The last thing she remembered was Earl uttering expletives under his breath.

Mabel glanced about the room. She did not know where she was and sat up suddenly. Dizziness threatened to overtake her again.

"I hope you're feeling better," Earl said. It appeared she was in his doctor's room. "Don't move too quickly, especially if you're still dizzy."

"I am a little," she said quietly, then wished she hadn't. She didn't want anyone fussing over her, especially Earl, who was trying to entice her to marry him.

"How long has this been going on?" He stared at her, then lifted her hand. "Your pulse is fast." She didn't need a doctor to tell her that. Her heart pounded so loudly she couldn't think straight.

Why had everything turned out so badly? She felt incredibly stupid not knowing Vern was such a horrible person. All those terrible things that happened back home, were they his doing? She took a deep breath, then sighed. It was now clear they were. Whatever bad things happened there, they would have been Vern's doing. No wonder he didn't want her wandering about. He didn't want her to see what he was up to.

Looking back now, she should have realized. He'd lied to her for far too long, and she'd believed him. Now, though, she had a target on her back.

"I haven't been unwell for long. Maybe a week." She studied him. Earl appeared concerned. He didn't know her, yet he was worried about her.

He scrubbed a hand across his chin. "What other symptoms do you have?"

Why should she tell him that? He wasn't her doctor. The thought made her pause. As of right now, he *was* her doctor, so she guessed she needed to cooperate. "I've been feeling nauseated, and sometimes vomited."

"In the mornings?"

Mabel nodded. "Do I have some terrible disease?" Maybe Vern wouldn't need to kill her after all. Whatever the disease she had, it would do the job.

Earl looked thoughtful. "I don't know how to say this, so I'll just come out and ask. Have you ever slept with a man?"

Mabel blinked back the tears that threatened to fall. "Vern, he…" She braced herself to utter the words. "He forced me. I had no choice." Her heart pounded, and she felt lightheaded again.

"I need to do an examination, but Mabel," he said grimly, "I think you might be with child."

"No! No, no, no!" she cried. Mabel covered her face with her hands and sobbed. "Not Vern's baby. Not like that."

Earl pulled her close and wrapped his arms around her. Mabel felt comforted, but it wasn't going to change the facts—she was an unmarried woman carrying a murderer's baby. She pushed Earl aside and tried to climb down off his examination table.

"Where are you going?" he asked as she fled.

She turned to face him. He appeared quite concerned. Where indeed? She had little money, no plans for the future, and a baby to support. "I have no idea," she whispered, and then she ran.

Mabel lay on the comfortable bed at the boarding house Earl had secured for her. She had cried so many tears, and was certain there were none left to cry, but she was wrong. The knock on the door set her off again. She prayed it wasn't Earl—as kind as he was, she didn't want to see him.

"Mabel, may I come in?" It was Earl. She should have known.

Should she allow him to enter her room? That was not appropriate, but she supposed with him being a doctor, no one would flinch.

Mabel sat upright on the bed. "I guess so," she said warily.

The door slowly opened, and he stepped inside, ensuring to leave the door open. She guessed that was for respectability. No one could make accusations that way. At least she presumed that to be the case.

"My offer still stands," he said as he sat in the chair next to her bed. "It's even more imperative now, don't you think?"

She stared into her lap where her hands were clasped. "I don't know," she whispered. "I'm very confused. My mind says no, since we're not in love, but my heart…" She sighed. "I have to think of my baby."

An almost imperceptible smile crossed his lips, but was gone as quickly as it had appeared. "That's settled then," he said, rubbing his hands together. "I'll go and talk to the preacher. You stay here and rest."

Just like that, he was gone. Mabel wasn't certain she'd made the right decision, but she was about to marry her groom's brother.

Chapter Four

What had he done? Earl hurried back home to break the news to Mrs. Halliwell. The older woman was ecstatic. Clearly, Mabel wasn't, but they both knew she could not support herself, let alone a child.

It would take a big adjustment, both for himself and for Mabel. But now, he had to get ready for his afternoon clinic. He had a full list and couldn't let his patients down. Some were minor ailments, and in those cases, what his patients really needed was company. Many were lonely, but if they wanted to pay for his time, then that was fine by him. Most were genuinely ill and needed his expertise.

The lonely patients were a concern, of course, but Earl wasn't sure how to solve the problem. The church ran activities all throughout the week. Perhaps he could discuss it with the preacher and come up with a resolution between them? No matter, it wasn't a problem he could solve at this very moment. He had more pressing things to worry about. Like Mabel and her unborn baby.

He strode into the waiting room to discover a horde of patients waiting for him. Earl didn't think he was late. He peered at his pocket-watch. He was almost fifteen minutes behind schedule. "Apologies, everyone. I had a pressing matter to attend to." He reached for the list of appointments and studied it. "Mrs. Gentry, please come in."

She stood and hurried into the surgery. "Good afternoon, Doctor," she said. "It's about the rash I have on my arms," she said once she was settled opposite the doctor.

Earl sighed. "I've told you, it's the soap you're using. Until you stop using it, the rash will remain." He stood then and went to a cupboard on the opposite side of the room. "Take this cream and use it twice daily. It will help relieve the rash, but unless you discard the soap in question, nothing will change."

Mrs. Gentry studied the container. "Thank you, Doctor," she said, and hurried out of the room. Normally, this sort of patient wouldn't worry him, but today? Today was different. He had genuine problems to think about. He crossed Mrs. Gentry off his list and read down the rest of the page. At least there weren't too many patients to see. He should be done in under two hours, and then he could visit the preacher.

Marrying Mabel was his top priority. Having her settled into her position as the doctor's wife was important. She needed to feel secure in her condition. It was very clear to Earl she was fragile. Not surprising, after all she'd been through.

"Mr. Cauldwell," he called, and the elderly gent hobbled into the room. At least this patient needed his help. "Climb up onto the examination bed, Mr. Cauldwell. What have you done to yourself?"

"I stumbled and was stood on by me horse," he said.

Earl had tried in vain to get the man to retire. With no heirs, who would run his farm? It was the same answer time after time. "I've had an idea, Mr. Cauldwell," the doctor said. "Have you thought of employing someone to run the ranch? Maybe promote your foreman to farm manager? You're far too old for this nonsense now." He stared sternly at the rancher, who rubbed a hand along his unshaven chin.

"By gosh," he said. "That might be worth looking into." The smile on the old man's face was reward enough for Earl. He only hoped the elderly man followed through.

Earl examined the offending foot. "Looks to be broken. I will bandage it, but it's a difficult place to splint. You're going to need crutches."

The other man groaned. "Are you sure, Doc?"

"I'm certain," Earl said. "I can lend you some crutches. Sit still while I bandage this up."

Cheryl Wright

Once the last of his patients left, Earl breathed a sigh of relief. It had been a particularly tough afternoon. Not because of his patients, but because of his state of mind. He still didn't really want to marry, but to be fair, Mabel had expected to be married by now. The least he could do was fulfill his brother's promise.

That didn't mean he had to be happy about it.

Earl pulled on the jacket of his best suit. He fiddled about with the tie far longer than should have been necessary. Doubts wracked his mind. He hadn't discussed it with Mabel, but this would be a marriage of convenience. Neither one of them wanted to marry, so there was no point making it out to be something it wasn't.

There was a tap on the door. "Mabel is ready, Doctor." Mrs. Halliwell had been a godsend. She'd taken Mabel to the mercantile to ensure she dressed appropriately for the wedding ceremony, as well as picking out a few suitable gowns for other use. It was apparent she would not fit into regular gowns for long, but they would deal with that when the time came.

After a final check in the mirror, he straightened his tie. At least it would be a private ceremony and there would be no curious onlookers. Mabel didn't need that. "I'll take Mabel to the church, shall I?"

the housekeeper asked. He supposed that was the right thing to do. The bride wasn't supposed to see the groom before the ceremony, but their situation was unique.

"I would appreciate it," he called through the door. Whatever his patients were going to think, he dared not to ponder. Then again, it was no one's business. Except his and Mabel's. The pair liked each other well enough, so the marriage should go smoothly. He would clear out the spare room for her once they were back.

He'd not brought up the subject of it being a loveless marriage yet—the poor girl had more than enough to worry about. Of course, she was a woman, but still very young. Her so-called fiancée must be a cad to have treated her in such a way. Earl couldn't even comprehend it.

Checking in the mirror once more, he determined it was time to leave. Why he felt so nervous about marrying Raymond's bride, Earl didn't know. He was certain Raymond would be very pleased with his brother for looking after the woman he promised to marry. But Earl wasn't sure *he* was thrilled. This would be a totally new experience for him. After all, he'd managed without a wife all this time.

He sighed. Best to stop ruminating and get to the church. Preacher Jones would not be happy at being kept waiting. It had been a last-minute arrangement, and he'd been very accommodating. Earl appreciated that.

Opening the door, he sighed again. It was now or never. Stepping outside his home, Earl looked at the sky. "I promise to look after her," he told his dead brother. "That doesn't mean I have to love it," he mumbled as he headed to the church. Almost immediately, Earl felt bad. He was a good person, a kind person, and his words did not hold him in good stead. Not even with himself.

In the blink of an eye, they were husband and wife. In her wisdom, Mrs. Halliwell had purchased a wedding ring for Mabel, and for that, he was very appreciative. The gown Mabel was wearing brought out the color of her eyes. When he thought about it, she really was beautiful.

Inside and out, he decided. Raymond would have been a very lucky man had he still been here. The thought made him pause. Did that mean *he* was a lucky man? Earl shook himself mentally. It was a marriage of convenience and nothing more. To the rest of the town, he would be the father of Mabel's baby. No one except his housekeeper would know another man fathered the baby. They would assume it came early. Besides, it was no one's business.

That was the problem with small towns like Pleasant Valley—everyone knew everyone else's business. At times, it was a good thing. The townsfolk would rally around and help when needed. Unfortunately, there were times a person wanted to keep their business private, and it was near impossible.

In other circumstances, his wedding would have been full of pomp and ceremony. Practically everyone from near and far would have attended. He preferred it this way. With the two necessary witnesses, Mrs. Halliwell and the preacher's wife, it was a quiet affair, and he was certain Mabel also preferred it that way.

"Should I go back to the boarding house now?" Mabel asked quietly once they were outside the church.

Mrs. Halliwell stared at her. "Absolutely not!" she said, clearly taken aback. "You are the doctor's wife, and must live in his residence." The housekeeper then turned to him and glared.

He wasn't the one to make the suggestion, so he wasn't sure why he'd earned her wrath. "No, of course not," he said firmly. "You will move here, as Mrs. Halliwell indicated." Should he mention the spare room? What would the older woman think about that? He shuddered to think. Perhaps he needed to rethink that particular idea.

"Doctor Carpenter will arrange that later. For now, it's time to celebrate. I've made a special supper for you both." She smiled and hurried toward the doctor's residence. Earl had enjoyed living there, but it had been lonely at times. He wasn't sure how much that would change now he was married, especially given there was no love involved.

He wondered how Mabel would feel about it, given he still hadn't brought the subject up. From what he understood, it's what she had before, so he had no doubt it would not differ from her previous relationship. Except this time, she wouldn't be locked away from the rest of the world.

He unlocked the door and opened it. Mrs. Halliwell stepped back and indicated at him.

What in the world? Did she really want him to carry Mabel across the threshold?

His wife would likely only marry once, so it was only fair to her, he guessed. He put his hands underneath her and scooped Mabel up. She was light as a feather. The smile she threw him was priceless. It was the first time he'd seen her smile since the moment she arrived, and it made his heart flutter.

Her arms went around his neck, and a zing went through him. This would never do. He did not want to have feelings for his wife. She was a complete stranger, and if it wasn't for the fact his brother had made a promise...

Her smile was infectious, and he smiled back. He hoped he wasn't being drawn into something he had no interest in.

Chapter Five

Mabel couldn't help but smile. Her new husband made her feel safe. He hadn't even flinched when he discovered she was pregnant. It made her wonder what Vern would have said when he found out she was having his baby.

A shudder went through her. She hoped and prayed he wouldn't come looking for her. She wasn't certain he would allow her to live if he did. After all, she did witness him murder a man. There was no excuse for what he did. She couldn't get the vision out of her mind. He held the gun to the defenseless man's head and pulled the trigger.

Even worse, he'd sniggered as he did it. A shudder wracked her very being.

"Are you alright, Mabel?" Earl's voice brought her back to the present. She needed to concentrate on the good things in her life. In her future, and her baby's future. She would not let Vern ruin her life. Had she stayed, that may very well have happened, but now, here with Earl, she had a chance at happiness.

He put her to the floor, and she turned to face him. "Just thinking, that's all." Trouble was, she was thinking about bad things, not the good stuff.

"You being unhappy is not good for the baby," Earl said matter-of-factly. She guessed that was the doctor coming out. He touched her arm, wrapped his fingers around it. "You're skin and bone. That's not good for the baby either. Mrs. Halliwell will fatten you up." He smiled then, and warmth flooded her whole body. Did her husband, a complete stranger, care about her? Or was it his doctor's side taking over? She had to admit it was probably the latter.

She seemed, somehow, to get herself into the most difficult situations. Perhaps that was because she had no guidance. Her parents were killed in an accident when she was quite young, and she'd been sent to an orphanage. Leaving the moment she was old enough—kicked out more like it—she'd met Vern only a few years later. He saved her from being destitute, clothed her, and looked after Mabel's every need. At the time, she believed he loved her.

She had certainly loved him.

And she'd believed every word he'd told her. She now understood how foolish she'd been. Mabel wished she was more worldly. Then she would have realized she was in a perilous situation. If she hadn't left her room that day, she would still be none the wiser.

Earl led her into the sitting room. "Why don't you sit here for a while? You look drained. Perhaps a cup of tea before supper?" He hurried into the kitchen before she had a chance to answer and returned soon afterwards with a cup of tea and a plate of biscuits.

"Thank you," she said quietly. Meekly. Why was she feeling so out of place? Earl was a nice person. A kind person. Mrs. Halliwell was wonderful. She was like the mother Mabel had never had.

"Mabel," Earl said almost gruffly, as she sipped her tea. "We need to discuss the… arrangements."

That made her ears prick up. "What arrangements?" Didn't they already do that? He married her, didn't he? Now she was confused. Mabel placed her teacup back on the saucer and sat back.

"The, er, sleeping arrangements. I have been thinking, and wonder if perhaps ours should be a marriage of convenience." He appeared more than a little uncomfortable. Earl loosened his tie and undid the top button of his pristine white shirt. "I will tidy up the spare room for you. That way, you'll have your privacy."

Mabel noticed Mrs. Halliwell standing in the doorway behind him. Earl had no view of the woman. She was furious. That much was clear. From her own perspective, Mabel was disappointed. She believed she was going into a proper marriage, not one based on responsibility. Tears flooded her face, and she ran from the room. Where she would go, she had no idea. Back to the church, to the preacher? Was it too late to get an annulment? She didn't think it was.

She slammed the front door behind her. The very spot where Earl had carefully carried her over the threshold not very long ago. Had she known then what she knew now, she would never have gone through with the marriage. She would have surely found a way to support herself and her child. Becoming a soiled dove was a last resort, but if it meant her baby would live, she would reluctantly do it.

"Mabel." Earl's voice carried across the road. She decided to go back to the boarding house. He'd paid for the night, so why not take advantage of it? In the morning, she would slip away quietly, and he'd never hear from her again.

It could work. Now she had a new name, Mabel Carpenter. Vern would never find her.

Yes, that would definitely work.

She began to run. Mabel lifted her skirts and took off. At first she ran along the boardwalk, then she slipped around the corner of a laneway in an effort to hide from her husband. What had she done to deserve such terrible treatment from the men in her life? Why did Raymond have to die before she arrived? From all accounts, Raymond would have been a wonderful husband. He would have taken care of her, and he didn't want a loveless marriage.

Mabel hiccupped on a sob, then resolved to compose herself. She couldn't think when she was upset, so leaned against the wall and took several deep breaths. Calmness suddenly overtook her, and she knew everything would be alright.

"There you are." It was Earl's voice—he was far closer than she would have liked. "I'm sorry," he whispered, and sounded genuine in his apology. "I truly am. I'm an idiot—Mrs. Halliwell told me I am, and she's always right." He grinned then, and Mabel couldn't help but smile, too.

Then she realized the depth of her situation. "I know I'm a burden, so I'm leaving." She had barely enough money for a train ticket to another town, but she would do it. She had to think of her baby.

The shock on Earl's face was palpable. "Please don't do that. I'll make an effort to be a good husband." He scrubbed a hand across his clean-shaven chin. "I want to take care of you. I truly do."

Her heart slammed against her chest. Should she listen, or should she run? Everything was happening far too quickly, and she couldn't think. She took another few deep breaths, then everything went black.

It was becoming a habit, this waking up on the examination table, and Mabel didn't like it one bit.

When she looked up, Earl stood over her, staring into her face. "You fainted," he said. "Hyperventilated, I think."

She stared at him. "You took too many deep breaths, and it made you lightheaded." Mabel nodded. He could be right. Earl pulled his stethoscope from around his neck and listened to her heart. Then he placed it on her belly. "You and the baby both seem to be fine." He threw her a tentative smile, then took her hand. "Can we start over? I don't know how to do this husband stuff. I've only ever been a doctor, and never had to think about anything else. Mrs. Halliwell does most of my thinking for me." He chuckled then.

It was rather endearing, but Mabel didn't want to be swayed by him. She needed to be clearheaded. The decisions she made from now on would affect both her *and* the baby, so she had to be certain of her choices.

"I've never had to think either," she whispered. "Vern did all that for me." She felt hollow. What should she do now?

Earl leaned over her, putting a hand behind one of her shoulders, then gently sat her up. "Dizzy?" he asked. She shook her head, and he helped her down the few steps and off the table. It seemed to Mabel when Earl was in doctor mode, he was a different person. He seemed to know what to do and how to do it.

It was Earl, the person, the husband, who had the issue with relating to people. It was the strangest thing.

"Perhaps we need to start from scratch," he said. Earl pulled his spectacles off his face and began to clean them. "I know it won't be easy. Neither of us knows the other, having met mere hours ago." He took a deep breath and then sighed. "Little did I know, back at the train station, you were here for my brother."

Mabel wasn't sure what to say. Or even if she should respond. Every time he spoke of Raymond, it was clear Earl became emotional. Not surprising since his brother was killed only days ago. It was upsetting to Mabel, and she didn't even know the man. She couldn't imagine how hard it was for her husband.

The thought made her pause. Her husband. Such a strange way to think, but Earl truly was her husband. Unless she arranged an annulment, which would be long and drawn out, he would stay as such.

They strolled into the sitting room again, and Mabel sat in the same chair she'd been in earlier. This time, Earl sat closer. "What are we going to do?" Mabel asked. She glanced down as she twisted her hands in her lap. "You don't really want me as your wife, and I only want somewhere safe for my baby and me."

Earl studied her far longer than was comfortable, and Mabel squirmed in her seat. "We'll make it work." She screwed up her face in disbelief, and his expression told her he'd noticed. Earl leaned over and took her hand. "I can't promise you anything," he said. "But I will do my darndest to make you happy and give your baby the best life possible."

Not one word he uttered convinced Mabel he would come to love her, or that he would even try. She closed her eyes for only a moment. In that instant, she resolved to build a life with Earl. It might not be a life filled with love, but it would be safe for her, as well as her child.

She was certain Earl would care for them both, but expecting any sort of relationship seemed far beyond what he was capable of. There was nothing she could do about it, so Mabel would simply have to accept the inevitable.

She glanced at Earl and smiled. "Thank you," she said quietly, and he squeezed her hand. The man wasn't devoid of emotion, but he certainly wasn't emotive either.

"That's settled then," he said, clapping his hands together. "This calls for a celebration." Earl grinned, then led her into the dining room, where Mrs. Halliwell was setting the table.

Chapter Six

Supper was wonderful. Not that he expected otherwise. Mrs. Halliwell was an excellent cook, and Earl had always been well fed and looked after properly.

Tonight, though, she'd outdone herself. Roast lamb, with mint sauce made fresh from his garden, along with roasted vegetables, also grown in his own yard. As a doctor, Earl pressed his patients to eat well, and tried to teach by example. Now he would try to convince Mabel to do the same thing. She was so thin and gaunt, and definitely needed to eat better, especially now she was pregnant.

This person who supposedly loved her, not only had he treated her badly, he also hadn't fed her properly. It made him angry. No, not angry, furious. He might not have known his fiancée was carrying a child, but it shouldn't have made a difference. Vern needed to care for her better.

He shook his head. It was water under the bridge now. Mabel was *his* wife, and he would ensure she was properly cared for. He would look after her the way she deserved. As for her baby, it was up to Earl to treat the baby exactly as he would if it were his own child.

"That was a wonderful meal, Mrs. Halliwell," Earl said sincerely. He glanced across at Mabel's plate. She'd barely eaten a bite. "Not hungry?" he asked, and she shook her head. It seemed clear she had been downtrodden for quite some time, and it bothered him. His first thought was how it could happen without her realizing. He'd seen it before, but not to this extent. Most of the time, the woman involved didn't know what was going on. The abuse happened over time until it became normal.

Mrs. Halliwell came back into the dining room, this time carrying her famous apple pie. She placed the pie in the middle of the table, along with a bowl of clotted cream. She smiled, then left them alone.

"Mabel," Earl said, and she glanced up at him. "You need to eat."

"I'm not hungry," she said, frowning. She sounded defeated.

"If you want your baby to survive, you must eat." Her eyes opened wide in surprise.

"Really?" she whispered. "My… my baby might die?" Tears filled her frightened eyes, and he realized she did not know about self-care.

"I'm afraid so," Earl said gently. "I will take care of you and the baby from now on. Mrs. Halliwell will ensure you get the food you require to carry a healthy child." His heart broke. Mabel wasn't old, but wasn't young either. He guessed she was around twenty-four, maybe a little older, but it was apparent she'd been sheltered from the real world. Keeping her away from other people hadn't helped her, but it was obvious Vern had done it to protect himself. Now Earl needed to protect her.

He dished out a slice of apple pie for each of them. "Cream?" She nodded, and he was pleased. At least it was dairy. He would encourage her to drink milk daily, as it was good for her child. Right now, marriage was new to them both. Tomorrow, they would begin a routine. Earl needed routines—it was the thing that kept him on time.

He needed to arrange a full complement of clothes and accessories for his wife. She needed so much, but it didn't bother him. Mabel was the doctor's wife, and that came with certain responsibilities. She especially needed to look the part.

As her belly grew, she would need maternity clothes. Perhaps the seamstress could help with that—he would get Mrs. Halliwell to make enquiries. In the meantime, though, he had to think about the sleeping arrangements. Apparently, relegating his new wife to the spare room was unacceptable.

Earl couldn't understand why.

Mabel emerged from the bathroom in her new flannel nightgown. No matter what she wore, his wife was beautiful. Out of respect for his dead brother, he had to keep those types of thoughts to himself. After all, Earl had only married her because of Raymond's promise of matrimony. Otherwise, he would have sent her on her way.

He shook his head. Earl knew that was untrue. He would never do such a thing. Especially not to someone as vulnerable as his wife. From the moment they met at the train station, it was clear there was far more to Mabel than could be seen on the surface. She was definitely in shock. He'd had no doubt, but there was so much more.

Not that he would tell her, but Earl was concerned about her former fiancée. From what she'd told him, Vern didn't seem like the sort of person to just let someone go. Especially after Mabel had watched him kill a man. More than likely, he was the type to hunt her down.

The thought sent shudders down his spine. Tomorrow he would talk to the sheriff—he would know what to do. At least Earl hoped he would. Right now, though, he needed to make his new wife feel comfortable. He would ease her into the position she now held—the doctor's wife. It was no easy feat to take on the position. At least, he'd heard that was the case. He'd had no experience himself until now.

"Did you enjoy your bath?" he asked with a smile. She looked terrified. Did Mabel think Earl would have his way with her? He wasn't barbaric, as her former fiancée had been. He would keep this as a marriage of convenience despite Mrs. Halliwell insisting they share a bed. This was an arrangement. He would look upon it as a business agreement of sorts.

Yes, that would work. For the both of them. Mabel needed a safe and stable home, and Earl's reputation certainly wouldn't be harmed by having a wife. He smiled again, then reached out and took her hand. "Feel better?"

She seemed wary. Of him? "It always helps to wash away the grime of the day." She smiled tentatively.

"You can have a bath every day if you like. Hot running water makes it easy." Pink flooded her cheeks, and he had a vision of her naked under the water. He shook himself mentally, then reminded himself this was akin to a business deal.

She yawned. "Sorry," she whispered.

He should have known she would be tired. She'd had a big day, not to mention all the travel she'd done, and in her condition, too. "It is getting late. I have a morning clinic tomorrow. Come on," he said, then led her to the bedroom.

Mabel glanced about curiously. "I've made space on this side of the closet," he said. "These drawers will be yours as well. I will arrange for more clothes and anything else you need." He almost added since you are the doctor's wife, but thought the better of it just in time.

Raymond would most certainly admonish him for thinking that way. He'd encouraged Earl to marry for some time, but Earl had resisted. A wife was the last thing he needed, he'd argued, stating his busy clinics and responsibilities to his patients. Raymond told him it was merely an excuse.

Was this his brother's way of getting back at him from beyond the grave? He almost laughed out loud at the thought.

Mabel glanced across the room at the bed. Mrs. Halliwell had placed clean sheets on it and had turned it back before she'd retired for the evening. His wife suddenly appeared terrified. It was then he remembered what she'd told him earlier, about being forced. "I promise not to touch you," he whispered, and she seemed to relax a little.

"Thank you," she whispered, then climbed into the freshly made bed. "Oh! Is this your side of the bed?" she asked, seemingly concerned.

He chuckled. "You can sleep wherever you like. I tend to move about as I sleep." He frowned then. "Hopefully, I don't infringe on your space." She didn't answer, and he wondered if it would bother her if he did. More likely than not, it would, but they would just have to see how it all worked out.

Earl began to undress, and she turned away. If it hadn't been such a difficult situation for them both, it might have been laughable. What she had endured was far from funny. He folded his clothes carefully and climbed in next to her. "Goodnight, Mabel," he whispered and closed his eyes.

He heard her gentle breathing and knew his wife was already asleep.

Earl awoke to find himself wrapped around Mabel. She was still sound asleep and was snuggled into him. He wasn't exactly unhappy about it, but neither did he want to make a habit of it. Sleeping this way was far from a marriage of convenience. He was a man, after all.

Add to that, his wife was beautiful. Things could quickly get out of hand if he let them. He vowed then and there not to let that happen. Now to extricate himself from Mabel without waking her. Earl gently removed each limb, one by one, as slowly and carefully as he could. Thankfully, Mabel didn't flinch, and didn't awaken.

Yesterday had been an awful day for her, and in her condition, that wasn't a good thing. She needed to rest, even if she resisted his help. He was her doctor and knew what was best for her and the baby.

He slid out of the bed, still trying not to wake her, then snatched up his clothes and headed for the bathroom. He would dress there rather than risk waking Mabel. She likely wouldn't appreciate his sneaking around her, but it was in her best interests.

He stepped out of the bathroom and bacon and eggs assaulted his sense of smell. It was *that* late? Normally, Earl would be awake at the crack of dawn. He preferred a leisurely breakfast, then going for a brisk walk before his clinic. He would also prepare for the clinic by pulling the file of each patient listed for that day. This despite being keenly aware of each patient and their ailments. Rarely did anyone new arrive in town.

"Good morning," Mrs. Halliwell said, standing in the kitchen's doorway. She glanced about. "No Mabel?"

"I'm letting her sleep," Earl said. "Her body could use the rest." He knew the moment he'd said the last words, he should have kept them to himself. Always thinking like a doctor, and never anything else. Mrs. Halliwell was constantly criticizing him for it.

This time, she didn't say a word. Instead, she glared at him. Her expression said it all. The problem was, Earl *was* a doctor. It was his life's work, and he'd never had to worry about anything or anyone else.

He spent far more of his time looking after patients, and little time away from his practice.

When he tended to Mabel at the station, he was meant to have the morning off. He honestly didn't know why he always scheduled a morning off once a week—he had nothing planned. But Mrs. Halliwell insisted he needed time for himself. She didn't factor in that Earl had no hobbies or interests outside of his medical practice. She'd tried to interest him in various activities, such as gardening. She even pushed him toward learning carpentry— there was a men's club at the church where he could do that, she'd told him.

None of it was to his liking.

He followed the housekeeper into the kitchen. "Sit," she said, indicating the breakfast table, then placed a mug of coffee in front of him. She turned away and dished out his breakfast, placing two slices of toast on the side of the plate. "Eat while it's hot. I'll take care of Mabel when she awakes."

"I appreciate that," he said, and truly meant it. Theirs might be a marriage of convenience, but he would still care for Mabel. Of course he would. He wouldn't have married her if he wasn't prepared to do the right thing by Raymond's bride.

Only Mabel wasn't Raymond's bride, she was *his* bride. Now all he needed to do was remember that.

Chapter Seven

Mabel woke up with a start. She glanced about, but it took a few seconds before she realized where she was.

Earl was gone. She reached out and felt the sheets— they were stone cold, which meant he'd been gone for some time. She quickly climbed out of bed and instantly regretted it. Dizziness overcame her, and she slumped onto the side of the bed. Mabel sat there for a few minutes until her lightheadedness disappeared.

Was this the way it would be the entire time she carried her baby? She hoped not. It wasn't the nicest feeling. She carefully stood and prepared to dress. It was then nausea surfaced. Bile rose in her throat and Mabel knew she was about to heave.

She ran for the bathroom, which thankfully wasn't far. How could this happen? She had so little in her stomach, and yet, here she was, emptying it out for all it was worth. Her eyes watered as she heaved. Her head ached, and she felt generally unwell.

When it was over, she felt a little better and washed her face with cold water.

Mabel heard footsteps running toward the bathroom. A knock at the door followed, and then Earl's voice. "Mabel, may I come in?" She wasn't sure what to do, and didn't answer. "Mabel?" He was certainly persistent.

"I guess so," she called through the door, which opened almost immediately.

"Mrs. Halliwell told me you were unwell." His hand went immediately to her forehead. "At least you don't have a fever. I believe this could be *morning sickness*." His grim expression didn't appease her.

"Morning sickness?" Mabel had never heard of it. "Am I going to… die from it?"

He chuckled then. "It's because you're pregnant. There's an easy cure."

Earl explained she needed to stay in bed each morning until she'd had a cup of tea and a piece of toast. That would help settle her stomach. Hopefully, the morning sickness would ease using that long-used method. Mabel certainly hoped so. It wasn't something she wanted to do every day, especially since Earl said it could last for weeks, or even months, in some cases.

Mabel splashed cold water on her face again, and her husband led her away from the bathroom. He guided her to the sitting room and went to arrange a light breakfast. "I must return to the clinic," he told her. "I have patients waiting. Will you be alright?" He appeared torn between staying with her and tending to his patients.

"I'm sure I'll be fine," she said. After all, her doctor was only a few doors away. She glanced up at the adjoining door that led into the clinic waiting room. "You go ahead."

He began to walk away, then stopped and turned back. "Are you certain? Mrs. Halliwell can fetch me if necessary."

She shrugged, and he continued on. For someone who demanded a marriage of convenience, he seemed overly concerned about her well-being. It was an unfortunate fact, but Earl cared more for Mabel as her doctor than he did as her husband. At least, that was the way she saw it.

It wasn't long before Mrs. Halliwell entered the room carrying a cup of tea and some toast. "Sip the tea, and eat the toast slowly," she said. "It's likely too late for today, but from now on, you are not to get out of bed until you've had your tea and toast."

"I promise," Mabel said, then reached for the tea. She took a careful sip—the last thing she wanted was to heave again.

Mrs. Halliwell studied her for a moment or two, then sat down in the chair next to her. "You'll have to forgive Dr. Carpenter," she finally said. "He's not very… personable." She straightened her back then. "Raymond was completely different—friendly and outgoing. The doctor has always been studious. His medical career has always come first. Relating to real people is difficult for him."

Real people? Did she mean anyone who wasn't a patient? Mabel had already discovered the reality of Mrs. Halliwell's statement. "He seems to be a good doctor," she said.

"He's an excellent doctor. There's none better." The older woman seemed determined in her assessment, and who was Mabel to argue? "Unfortunately, he's not good with anyone who is not a patient." She reached across and squeezed Mabel's hand. "Give him time. I'm hoping having a wife will bring him out of his shell."

That was a big goal Mrs. Halliwell had placed on her shoulders. Mabel wasn't certain she was up to it.

The housekeeper stood then. "I must prepare the soup and bread for lunch. Will you be alright?" She looked genuinely concerned, and for that, Mabel was grateful.

"I'm certain I will be. Thank you," she said, and the older woman smiled at her, and then was gone.

It left Mabel alone to ponder her new life. Right now, she wanted to lie down and sleep. Earl had already told her rest was important in her condition, but she didn't want to sleep her days away. She'd been forced to do that when Vern ran her life. At least with Earl, she was free to roam the town as she pleased.

She finished up her tea and toast and took her dishes to the kitchen. Mabel already felt better. Instead of hanging around here and doing nothing, she dressed and fixed her hair. After that, she informed Mrs. Halliwell she was going to look around Pleasant Valley. The housekeeper looked terrified.

Mabel browsed the mercantile, noting the variety of gowns they carried, and checking the unmentionables, soaps, and shoes. Apart from the gown bought for the wedding ceremony, and a few additional gowns purchased at the time, she had nothing but the clothes on her back and her reticule. It wasn't the way Mabel had chosen to start married life.

Vern had promised her the world. That was before Mabel knew who he really was. It was still hard to believe she'd watched him kill a man. In cold blood. And for what? Mabel would probably never know. She should have realized there was more to Vern than she understood. He was secretive, and easy to anger. Mostly he was kind to her, except when he...

She didn't want to think about that. Why didn't she run after the first time? Probably because there was nowhere to run. She had little money, and it was hard to get away. Escaping Vern had been difficult, not to mention stressful. She'd had to change from train to stagecoach along the way. Mabel was lucky to escape with her life. No longer did she believe Vern loved her. Rather, she now understood he probably wanted her dead. At least here in Pleasant Valley, with a new name and a new identity, he wouldn't be able to find her.

"Go ahead and choose some gowns," Mrs. Halliwell told her.

Mabel was reluctant to buy anything. Spending Earl's money wasn't the goal; she simply needed to get out of the house and into the fresh air. Still, there were a lot of beautiful things here at the mercantile. She gravitated to the area where the undergarments were kept. She needed to buy more of those, some stockings, and definitely another gown or two. Being repeatedly told she was the doctor's wife and needed to look the part didn't appease Mabel. She did, however, concede it was the truth. Soon she would need maternity garments, and the housekeeper said she would arrange for a fitting when the time came. It wouldn't be for some weeks, though.

In the meantime, Mabel was enjoying pottering about and finding various items the store carried. In all her adult years, she'd never been allowed to simply wander about. Vern was always with her wherever she went, and he decided what she could and couldn't have.

She felt like a child in a candy store.

Mrs. Halliwell assisted Mabel in choosing the clothes and other items she needed, and carried them to the front counter. On the walk there, Mabel came across perfumed soap. The fragrance of lavender enticed her toward them. Her mother had a huge lavender bush at the front door when Mabel was growing up, and it reminded her of happier days. Back then, she was wanted. Her parents loved her, but once they were gone, life was never the same.

She braced herself and walked away. "We'll also have four cakes of the lavender soap," she heard Mrs. Halliwell say. Mabel knew it was futile to argue. The housekeeper had the final say—on everything. Even Earl knew that. That her husband was told what to do by his housekeeper was rather amusing to Mabel, but it was very clear he was not always capable of making life decisions. "Anything else you need, Mabel?" Mrs. Halliwell's voice brought Mabel out of her musings.

"I don't think so," she answered. Soon she would have to think about baby clothes and diapers. Even furniture for the baby. Mabel wasn't certain Earl was ready to announce her pregnancy yet. More likely, there would be no announcement. Although it was impossible to keep something like that a secret. Not once her belly grew.

"We can deliver that for you," the mercantile owner said. "It's far too cumbersome for you lovely ladies to carry."

"Thank you, Clyde. It would be appreciated." They hurried away once each item was written into the accounting book.

Once outside, Mrs. Halliwell took Mabel to another store. They stood outside as the older woman studied the items displayed in the window. "I don't need boots," Mabel protested, but the truth was, she had only one pair. They weren't in terrible condition, but they also wouldn't be suitable for church. They were still usable, but beginning to show wear.

Mrs. Halliwell pulled her lips into a tight line and went inside. Mabel followed behind. "Good morning, Harold," she greeted the bootmaker. "We need boots for Mrs. Carpenter."

The man raised his eyebrows. "The doc's married? Never thought the day would come." He chuckled, then turned away after studying Mabel's current boots. "These might work. I'll need you to take off the boots you're wearing," he said, indicating for

Mabel to sit down. He sat down on a chair opposite her, that seemed perfect for what he was doing.

Once her shoes were off, the bootmaker measured her feet, then told Mabel to try the boots he'd shown her. They were a perfect fit, as he'd believed they would be. "They're very comfortable," Mabel told him, as she walked around the room.

"Harold is the finest bootmaker in all the county," Mrs. Halliwell said matter-of-factly. She wandered around the store, checking the various styles. "We'll take this style in Mabel's size as well."

"I don't have them in stock, but can have them ready by tomorrow afternoon." With the order placed, and the account finalized, they left the store with Mabel proudly wearing her new boots.

"You look tired," Mrs. Halliwell told her as they headed home. "A nice cup of tea and a rest will do you good."

Mabel nodded and happily headed back to the doctor's house. Her new home, she suddenly realized.

Chapter Eight

"You did what?" Earl demanded, when he returned from his morning clinic. It wasn't that he didn't trust her. It was nothing like that. His concern was if the wrong people saw her. Like her former fiancée. Mabel had assured him Vern wouldn't come looking for her, but Earl had his doubts. Anyone who killed a man in cold blood was capable of anything.

It was time to visit the sheriff, despite Mabel's protests. Once his afternoon clinic was over, they would go to the sheriff's office and let him decide if Mabel was in danger or not.

"You can't keep her locked up," Mrs. Halliwell growled. "The poor girl has spent most of her adult life living like a prisoner. And you want to do the same?"

Earl ran a hand across his chin. "Not at all," he said, feeling a little more calm. "I want to keep her safe. Until we can talk to the sheriff, I believe Mabel should stay put."

He glanced across at his wife, who was currently pursing her lips. She was far from happy. Was this to be their first argument? He hoped not. She had enough angst in her life.

"I might be your wife, but you can't keep me locked up like Vern did." She was firm in her statement, and Earl could see she was furious. He'd not told either woman Mabel was to stay put, so it was all his fault. Honestly, he didn't think he needed to tell either of them. His wife's life was in danger, and she needed protection. Did Mabel not understand that?

He studied her. Mabel sat in the comfortable chair, her hands twisting in her lap. Somehow, he needed to fix this. "Your new boots are pretty," he said offhandedly. She glared at him. Not the greeting he'd expected on coming home for lunch. The clinic had been a busy one today, lots of genuine ailments, which he always found easier to deal with.

Mrs. Halliwell stood. "I'll serve lunch. If you don't eat soon, you won't have time to eat before your patients begin arriving again," she told him firmly.

Of course, she was right. The housekeeper always knew best. Earl relied on her far too much. Now he was married, he needed to make decisions for himself. He didn't want his new wife to believe him to be weak, or heaven forbid, stupid.

He was far from that. Earl knew he was. The truth was, he preferred to use his brain power for medical decisions. It's where his strengths lie, and he had always kept to his strengths. It seemed perfectly legitimate to him.

Earl stood and reached a hand to Mabel. She pushed it away, then stood on her own. Was his wife defiant? He doubted Vern would have put up with unacceptable behavior. No, she was angry with him. She'd obviously had a wonderful time shopping, and he'd ruined it for her.

"I'm sorry," he said, reaching for her hand again. This time she glanced up at him, which was more than she'd done before. "I am worried about your safety. I don't want to lose you," he whispered. He kept his hand outstretched until finally she allowed him to grip her hand. Once standing, he pulled her close and wrapped his arms around her. Mabel didn't resist. In fact, she relaxed into his chest. It surprised Earl at how good it felt to hold her close.

What would his brother think of him holding Mabel this way?

Earl could envisage Raymond looking down and smiling. "Finally," he would be saying. Earl knew it to be true.

"We should have lunch," Earl said quietly, and Mabel glanced up at him. Her face had softened, and she appeared happier now.

"I'm sorry," she whispered. "I didn't think going out would be a problem. Don't be angry at Mrs. Halliwell—she tried to stop me."

He harrumphed. Earl should have known the housekeeper would take care of his wife. Why he'd thought to blame her, he didn't know. And why he was so upset was equally puzzling. He'd known Mabel for a little over twenty-four hours and already felt endeared to her.

It was pure stupidity. The only thing he could think of was Raymond had made her a promise. There could be no other feasible explanation. He gently pushed Mabel away and immediately regretted it. There had been comfort in holding her, but he doubted his wife felt the same. She appeared unaffected by the movement, but for him, it was different. Now he felt hollow, as though something was missing.

He couldn't fathom what that could be.

As they ate lunch, Mabel chatted about her visit to the mercantile. She told him about the things she'd bought, and those she hadn't but caught her eye. It was very clear Mabel had been imprisoned for far too long. She may not have seen it that way, but in reality, she had been a prisoner to her former fiancée. Just the thought of that so-called man made Earl's blood boil.

Still, he worried about his wife wandering about town. It was unlikely, but what if Vern found her? Earl had absolutely no doubt Mabel would be in danger. If Vern had a history of killing in cold blood, as she had witnessed, he was capable of murdering Mabel to keep her quiet.

He glanced across the table as she chatted. Mrs. Halliwell sat with them, and it was clear she was concerned too. The housekeeper had been with him for some years, and Earl could read her like a book.

He needed to speak with the sheriff sooner rather than later.

"The aroma was so lovely."

Aroma? What was she talking about? Earl needed to stop woolgathering, and start listening to his wife.

"The soap." She sounded a little annoyed. What else had he missed? "They had lots of different fragrances. It was like walking into a garden filled with flowers." Her expression was one of pure happiness. Earl would store that for future reference.

"That sounds good," he said, and she smiled. It appeared it didn't take much to make Mabel happy. He would also remember that. Perhaps small gifts here and there would be appropriate. From what he could tell, she'd been deprived... of just about everything that made her happy. The small things seemed important to her, like fragrant soap.

The trouble was, he'd never dealt with this sort of thing before. He'd never had a girlfriend—he was too busy studying to be a doctor for that type of nonsense. Once he had his degree, he was too busy with his practice. Granted, his first practice was small. Well, his part of it was. He was in partnership with a more seasoned doctor, which at the time suited him, but it became apparent he was being given the less important ailments to deal with.

It was then he decided to branch out on his own. The thought was quite frightening at first, but the people of Pleasant Valley had quickly made him feel at home. Earl's hope was they would do the same for Mabel. She was a friendly person once she let her guard down, but also seemed far too trusting. If she told anyone of her situation, in a place like this, word would spread like wildfire.

"Mabel," he suddenly said, "don't talk to anyone about your past." She frowned at him. "About Vern, I mean."

"I don't understand," she told him.

"People around here, they… gossip. Whatever you say will get passed on. Before you know it, everyone in town will know."

"Oh."

"I'll talk to the sheriff and work out a plan to keep you safe."

Mrs. Halliwell nodded her approval.

"In the meantime, don't go anywhere." He studied her. "You have everything you need for now, don't you?"

"For now," Mrs. Halliwell said firmly. "The seamstress will be needed in a few weeks. There is no way around it."

Earl knew what she meant. Mabel's baby bump would be visible in a few weeks. Hopefully, by that time, all this worry about Vern would be in the past, and he could rest easy, knowing she was safe.

Raymond would want it that way.

As he stood to return for the afternoon clinic, Earl realized *he* wanted it that way. The more time he spent with Mabel, the more endeared he became to her. She was a gentle soul, and from what he had seen so far, cared about others. It was a terrible shame she'd been treated so badly.

That was changed now. He was her husband, after all.

Earl sat across the desk from Sheriff Amos Charleston, Mabel by his side.

The sheriff leaned back in his chair and fiddled with the pencil in his hand. "This man, Vern… what was his name?" He frowned then, and Earl realized he wasn't taking it seriously.

He heard Mabel sigh. "I watched him murder a man," she said, fury clear in her voice. "If you think this is a joke, you are very wrong." Mabel stood and turned away, ready to leave.

She glanced around the room at the *wanted* posters. Her expression changed from annoyance to astonishment, then in only a few steps, stood in front of the wanted posters. Her shaking fingers pointed to one poster in particular. She then glared at the sheriff. "That's him. That's Vern. I watched him murder that cowboy. Who knows how many other men he killed?"

Before either of them could say a word, Mabel stormed out of the sheriff's office. Earl turned to the sheriff, a man he barely knew. "Are you happy now?" he said as calmly as he could muster, then followed his wife, ensuring she was safe.

As he left the room, Earl heard the sheriff's chair screech. Presumably, he was checking out that poster.

"Mabel," he called to her retreating back. "Wait up." He glanced about, ensuring no one was around to see them. More importantly, to see Mabel.

He strolled across the street, his legs far longer than hers, and caught up quickly. "He'll come around. Now he knows exactly who he's dealing with."

She suddenly stopped walking. "He treated me like the village idiot," she said, her eyes piercing him. He hadn't seen Mabel like this before. Not that he blamed her. It had taken courage to open up to the sheriff, and the lawman had mocked her.

Now there was proof of how dangerous Vern was, and what he was capable of. Surely the sheriff would act? Earl knew one thing, and one thing only—Mabel was his wife, and he was responsible for her safety. He had to take care of her, no matter what.

Chapter Nine

Days later, Mabel was still fuming. Sheriff Amos Charleston had absolutely no idea of what Vern was capable of doing. She knew he would come after her, not that she would let on to Earl she thought he would.

The Vern she had known for years wasn't the same man she'd seen murder a cowboy without flinching. That Vern was a vicious killer. A cruel man who wanted to watch his victim squirm until the last second. The fact she'd witnessed that didn't sit well with Mabel, but she was glad she finally saw her former fiancée's true color. Saw him for what he truly was—a cruel man who cared little for anyone else.

How she had been so naïve, and for so long, she did not know. Mabel had tried to rest. It had been days since their futile talk with the sheriff, but it had completely drained her. Earl had done his best to console her, but it hadn't worked. It was clear to Mabel he was as concerned as she was.

As she tried to sleep, there was a knock at the front door. She heard footsteps, and then Earl's muffled voice. After a short time, the door closed. Shortly after, Earl was in the bedroom. He sat on the side of the bed before he spoke. She appreciated him not towering over her.

"The sheriff is here," he explained. "He apologized for not taking you more seriously, and wants to talk to you."

Mabel didn't respond immediately, and instead studied her husband. "Well, I don't want to talk to him," she said, then rolled away so her back was to Earl. She knew she was being childish, but she was still angry with the sheriff.

She was startled when Earl touched her cheek. "Mabel? It's important, don't you think?" She knew he was right, but it didn't particularly calm her down. Never had she felt fury build inside her as she had at the sheriff's office. The man was a fool for not believing her. And she would tell him so.

She slowly rolled back to face him, then carefully sat up. Mabel did not want to become lightheaded again. It wasn't a pleasant feeling. "I need to fix my hair," she said as she stood.

"Your hair is fine. You're only putting off the inevitable."

Earl was right. She knew he was. Mabel had to face the sheriff—if not now, then later, so she might as well get it over and done with. She nodded curtly, and headed into the sitting room, where she was sure Earl would have left him. Knowing Mrs. Halliwell, he would have a mug of coffee in his hand.

The moment she entered the sitting room, Mabel felt herself stiffen. This lawman, who was meant to uphold the law, had taken it upon himself to dismiss her out of hand. He clearly hadn't believed a word she told him. That is, until she was able to identify Vern from a wanted poster. Although that wasn't the name shown on the poster. It was not a name she recognized.

"Sheriff," Mabel said curtly as she stepped into the room. She then sat down opposite him. "What can I do for you? Clearly it's nothing to do with Vern, since you didn't believe a word I told you." She glared at him, then wondered what her husband thought of her antics. Glancing across at Earl, she noticed him grinning behind his hand. Perhaps he approved of her stance after all.

"Mrs. Carpenter," Amos said, pink coloring his cheeks. "I apologize profusely for my behavior. I've done some digging, and it has since come to light that what you've said is true."

His statement did not appease her. The man was literally calling her a liar. "So I'm a liar?" she snapped, then stood to leave.

Amos looked confused. "I… I didn't mean it that way. We always have to check these things."

Earl came to her side, no doubt hoping to convince Mabel to stay and hear the sheriff out.

"Just because you don't know him under that name doesn't mean he isn't a killer," she said. "You obviously have an issue with women."

Earl put an arm around her and gently guided her back into her seat. Mabel had surprised herself. She had never been a forthright person. Never had she gone on the offensive. Perhaps because she was afraid of the consequences. But not anymore. Now she had to protect herself and her baby. Now she needed to ensure Vern didn't get to her. She was certain if he found her, he would destroy her.

Mabel hated to think that way, but it was no longer only herself she had to worry about. She now had a baby to concern herself with as well. She'd vowed not to think of it as Vern's baby and hoped he never found out. Otherwise, knowing what Vern was like, he would fight to take his child away from Mabel. It was the last thing she wanted.

The sheriff's face reddened even more than before. He flustered for what seemed an eternity, then unrolled a large piece of paper. He suddenly shoved an unraveled wanted poster toward her. "Is this the man you call Vern?"

She studied the image—it was Vern. There was absolutely no doubt in her mind. She knew him intimately, and had done so for some years. "That's him." Mabel scanned the activities he was wanted for—murder, robbery, kidnapping, and so much more. She swallowed hard. How had she not realized what Vern really was? It was difficult to comprehend the Vern she'd known compared with the criminal portrayed on the wanted poster before her.

"With that confirmed," Earl said, his voice a little shaky, "what are you doing to protect my wife?" His last words were said firmly and with conviction. They also held emotion.

It seemed rather strange to Mabel, but these past days, they had gotten to know each other better. She had felt more comfortable in her new surroundings, and with her new husband. They had even consummated their marriage, which had not bothered her. Earl was coming out of his shell over the past days. He was such a gentle person, a caring person. He was making decisions instead of relying on Mrs. Halliwell. Mabel could see the housekeeper was pleased with the turn of events.

Amos cleared his voice. "I believe your wife is safe. I gather *Vern* does not know where you are?"

Mabel's eyes opened wide in astonishment. "I certainly hope not. I didn't tell him if that's what you mean. I had to sneak away without him knowing."

"The truth is, Sheriff," Earl interrupted, "in case you've forgotten, my wife witnessed a violent murder. I can't imagine the killer wants her to relay the story."

Mabel gasped. Earl glanced across at her. "I'm sorry, my darling," he said gently, and reached for her hand. "Amos doesn't seem to understand how grave your situation is."

She nodded, but knew she had paled. It was confirmed when Earl suggested she lie down for a while. As she left the room, Mabel heard Earl explain she was unwell and needed to rest. It wasn't long before the sheriff left and all was quiet again. Finally, she closed her eyes and slept.

Chapter Ten

Earl paced the sitting room while Mabel slept. She needed the rest; he knew she did. The sheriff's visit had not appeased any of his worries. His wife was still in danger and Amos had no intention of doing anything about it.

If only he knew *what* to do, Earl would make it happen. Money was no object—he didn't care what it cost. They hadn't been together long, but he had feelings for Mabel, and they got stronger by the day.

It seemed rather ridiculous, as only a week ago they were complete strangers, but Mabel had endeared herself to him quickly. He'd tried his best to keep her at arm's length, but it hadn't worked. At first, he felt sorry for her and convinced himself that's all there was to it. But as the days rolled on, he came to realize there was far more to it.

Once she'd opened herself up to him, everything changed—for both of them. Once they had consummated their marriage, a far greater connection seemed to take over. All that despite his pledge to keep it a marriage of convenience. Why he ever thought that could occur, he didn't know. He was obviously kidding himself.

"What is wrong with you?" Mrs. Halliwell demanded as she strode into the sitting room with a tray of coffee, tea, and cake.

Earl put his fingers to his lips. "Mabel is sleeping." He sat down then and snatched up the mug of coffee and a slice of the lemon cake. "Thank you. This is delicious," he said when he'd eaten a mouthful.

"What are you doing to protect your wife?" she demanded again. "I gather that's your problem."

She studied him, and as always, saw right through him. "I don't know what to do, and the sheriff seems to think she'll be fine." He shook his head. "I don't agree." Earl took another sip of his coffee and choked as though swallowing down stones.

Mrs. Halliwell walked over and pounded on his back. "I'm worried too," she said, then walked away once he stopped coughing. But not before he saw the tears swimming in her eyes. In all the years she'd worked for him, never had he seen her so upset.

Shortly afterwards, Mabel woke from her nap. She came into the sitting room and sat near to him. "Just in time," Earl said, far more cheerfully than he felt. "Mrs. Halliwell brought in tea and cake for you."

Mabel rubbed at her eyes. She appeared a little better now than she had earlier. There was even color in her cheeks. Glancing over the tray, she lifted the tea, then helped herself to the cake. "This is good," she said with a smile. It warmed Earl's heart to see her happy. He loved when she smiled, which wasn't often. If he could eliminate the threat, she could be truly happy.

"How are you feeling?" Earl asked, then could have kicked himself. Mabel had told him he behaved more like a doctor than a husband, but he was truly concerned for her health. Neither Mabel nor the baby had a good start. Since she'd arrived, his wife was looking more healthy, which wasn't surprising since she was eating far better now.

"I'm tired, but fine." She smiled tentatively, and Earl was sure she was concerned.

He reached out and lifted her hand. "It's the stress, I'm certain," he said, then kissed her hand. Mabel's eyes opened in surprise. He was trying hard to be the sort of husband she deserved, but still had a lot to learn.

She glanced at him over the top of her teacup. Taking another sip, she then nodded. "I know. I have always slept a lot, mostly out of boredom. But it's different now. There are things I can do here— like helping Mrs. Halliwell."

Earl frowned. He didn't want Mabel doing too much. She was fragile and needed to rest. He also understood she wanted to do things and not spend her days doing nothing. "Not too much, I hope?"

"Mrs. Halliwell won't let me do much. I set the table, and we go to the mercantile together."

He nodded his understanding, but still wasn't certain the mercantile was a good place for Mabel to be. Having her out in public was a risk he'd rather not take. He was taking the complete opposite stance from the sheriff. Unlike Sheriff Charleston, Earl assumed his wife was still in danger. "Please be careful." He didn't want to scare her, nor did he want Mabel to feel the danger was over. Until her former fiancée was behind bars, he wouldn't feel comfortable.

"I am, I promise. Mrs. Halliwell has been taking good care of me," she said, curiosity in her voice.

Had Mabel suddenly realized exactly how concerned he was? Earl needed to be far more careful with the information he shared and the way he dealt with Mabel. Danger abounded, and he didn't want her exposed to it.

She finished up her tea and placed the cup carefully in the saucer. "I'd like to go for a stroll," Mabel said, studying him. After the conversation they'd just had, did she expect him to say no? That was, of course, his immediate response, but Earl understood she needed to get outside in the fresh air. The exercise would do her good as well. It would also help relieve her stress. And his.

"Why not?" he said as he stood, then reached out for Mabel's hands. She was beaming, and it warmed his heart. Staying close to home, and in public places, would be best. If they went somewhere isolated, like the gazebo, it would leave them wide open for attack. "Would you like to visit our church gardens? We didn't get the chance when we were there last." That was the day they married, and by the time they left the grounds, it was dusk. "It's quite beautiful there, and I'm sure you'd enjoy it. There's even a bench to rest on."

Mabel put her hands to her heart. "That sounds wonderful. Let me freshen up, and I'll be back shortly."

Earl drank down the last of his coffee as he watched his wife's retreating back. Being with her filled his heart with joy. If only the worry about her safety wasn't a factor, they could be truly happy. He was certain of it. With a baby coming, they would soon be a family, and perhaps one day, they would have children together. If only Mabel had feelings for him, things could be different.

Mabel breathed in the fragrance of the flowers surrounding them and smiled. She seemed to relax here in the garden, and it pleased Earl. He would bring her here more often. The stroll to the church property was an easy walk for them both, and they could wander throughout the garden to their heart's content.

The ladies' auxiliary met once a week to tend to the multitude of flowers, and did a magnificent job. Perhaps one day, when things were settled, Mabel might even join them. Earl could picture her here— watching her now, he was certain she would be in her element.

"It is so beautiful here," she exclaimed, her voice full of excitement. "Can we come here every day?"

Earl grinned as he watched her breathe in the fragrance surrounding them. "We can. Perhaps after breakfast each morning. You could join me on my morning stroll."

Mabel appeared confused. "Of course," he said with sudden understanding. "You're usually in bed having your tea and toast. We will find a time that is suitable for us both." He hooked her arm through his, and they moved to another part of the gardens where a wooden bench sat. It was surrounded by a variety of flowers—prairie coneflowers, echinacea, and more. A Sycamore tree and a Red Maple overshadowed the flowers. The shade was welcomed after the heat of the sun.

When he glanced at Mabel, Earl noticed she had far more color in her face. She wasn't as pale as she was when they'd left home. Her eyes appeared brighter, and she seemed far happier. If she wasn't so thin, you wouldn't know she'd been unwell.

"What are you staring at?" Mabel asked, concern wracking her voice. "Is something wrong?"

Earl shook his head. "Absolutely nothing is wrong. I am pleased at how well you now look. And how happy you seem here."

"I adore it here," she said, her voice almost a whisper. She opened her mouth to say more, but clamped her lips shut. It made Earl wonder what she was about to say.

He pulled his pocket-watch out and checked the time. "Can you believe we've been here almost an hour? Perhaps we should leave. I'd hate for you to get a chill."

Mabel seemed to deflate at his words. "A little longer," she pleaded. "It's so peaceful here, and I'm not cold, I promise. I haven't been to church for such a long time, and I feel close to God here in his beautiful garden."

There was no way Earl could say no. That Mabel had been deprived of the chance to attend church was unthinkable. He settled back on the wooden bench and enjoyed the happiness the garden brought to his wife.

To top off what had been a wonderful visit, Preacher Jones came out to the garden and sat with them. Earl noticed the way Mabel's face lit up as she chatted to the preacher. He talked to her about the ladies' auxiliary, and some tasks they did around the church. Listening to their conversation, it was clear Mabel craved being with other women her age. It was an unfortunate fact it couldn't happen.

At least not until Vern was found and jailed. That was a day Earl looked forward to, but not at the expense of his wife's safety and well-being.

Chapter Eleven

Mabel enjoyed their time in the garden. Walking through the church garden had felt exhilarating. Sitting on the wooden bench, surrounded by the fragrant plants, a peacefulness had come over her.

She was ecstatic when Preacher Jones arrived. The mere act of sitting with him made her feel better. Talking to him, even for a short time, quelled her anxiety. Mabel knew she wanted to do it far more often.

Until now, she'd felt anxious. In the back of her mind was Vern. The worry was he would turn up out of nowhere. When that happened, she knew the result. He would ensure she couldn't relay what she'd witnessed. Little did he know it was already too late.

Now she'd relayed his whereabouts to the sheriff, Mabel knew Vern would eventually be captured and hanged. With the information she'd provided, the sheriff was certain he would be located, but Mabel, not so much. It was obvious Vern was as cunning as a rat. If he thought she'd revealed his whereabouts, he would move on and settle in another unsuspecting town. He would eventually turn it into another Hell's Gate. The town she'd had to flee to save her life.

Preacher Jones patted her hand that he'd previously held, as if he knew she needed a distraction. "I must leave you now," he said. "We'll talk again next time you visit."

Mabel smiled. She had enjoyed their time together.

She'd promised herself to enjoy her time here in the gardens, and she'd done exactly that. With Earl by her side, how could she not? Despite living in town, and not isolated on the ranch where Raymond would have taken her, she felt happy.

It made her wonder what Raymond had been like. From what Mrs. Halliwell told her, he was far more forthright than Earl. He liked people and was fun to be around.

Earl, on the other hand, was quiet, and didn't particularly like spending time with people, apart from his patients. Mabel had noticed a change in him since she'd arrived, so that was something. She was beginning to know who she was as well. Instead of being forced to do whatever Vern wanted, she was able to make decisions of her own. That was important to Mabel—in her short life, she'd had little choice about anything that would affect her.

At every step, someone else had dictated how she would live. As a woman, she had few choices in life, but no longer under Vern's control, she hoped to have some input into how she lived her life.

"We should go," Earl said, reaching for his pocket-watch. "It's almost suppertime. Mrs. Halliwell won't be pleased if we are late."

Mabel chuckled. "She certainly won't. She's a stickler for punctuality."

Earl raised his eyebrows. "You've noticed that already? I guess it's not difficult to see." He helped Mabel to her feet, and they headed back home. "Our visit here seems to have done you a lot of good," he told her, as he hooked his arm through hers.

"I feel a lot better," Mabel said. It was true—perhaps all she needed was fresh air and to be surrounded by nature. That it was God's garden was even better. She felt so much more at peace in this place. Of course, it had to end. They couldn't stay here forever, more's the pity. She could see herself spending far more of her time here. Now that she knew it existed, Mabel wanted to come here regularly.

"You have rosy cheeks," Earl said, and ran a finger down one cheek. Mabel liked when he touched her. When he was acting as her husband, and not her doctor. As the latter, he was very matter-of-fact, and portrayed little emotion. Only Mabel had seen the other side of Earl. The intimate side of him. He was a considerate man. Very caring of Mabel and her feelings.

The pity of it all was he had no true feelings for her. It seemed silly, after such a short time, but Mabel was developing feelings for her husband. For him, it was an obligation he felt he had to fulfill. For Mabel, it was entirely different.

For the first time in a long time—years in fact—someone truly cared for her. Whether that was out of obligation or something else entirely, it didn't matter. Earl thought she was worth the effort. Unlike Vern, who treated her like his possession. Someone to boast about, and to treat like his toy.

Mabel flinched at the memory. She'd hoped it would be the only time, except it wasn't. She was available at his will, and there wasn't a thing she could do about it. She now realized it was only one of the reasons Vern kept her locked away from the world.

She only wished her baby could have been made out of love. Earl had promised to take care of them both, and treat her baby like his own. She wasn't convinced. Few men would accept another man's child as their own.

The front door opened before Earl had even reached for the handle. "You both look happy. Relaxed." Mrs. Halliwell smiled.

"We've been to the church gardens," Mabel offered. "It's beautiful there."

"That explains it. The gardens are very special."

The housekeeper smiled at her then, and Mabel felt as though she'd come home. Whether it was her time in the garden, or whether she finally felt she fit in, Mabel wasn't sure. Until now, she'd felt like an intruder in a previously serene home. Her inclusion had changed everything for both Earl and the kindly Mrs. Halliwell.

She didn't want that. Didn't intend to upset the balance they had there. Earl seemed happier than he did when she arrived, but it could be he'd simply become used to having her there.

"Mabel?" Earl's voice cut through her reflections and brought her back to reality. "Where did you go?" he asked as he chuckled. He put a hand to her back and led her into the dining room. The table had already been set, and Mrs. Halliwell was in the kitchen, dishing out the food.

Mabel breathed in the aroma of their supper. Earl grinned. "It smells delicious," he said, then moments later, their food was placed in front of them. "Lamb stew, and freshly baked bread," Mrs. Halliwell said, then hurried out of the room.

"She never stops," Mabel whispered.

Earl agreed. "You are right. She is on the go all the time. I have practically begged her to slow down, but she never does."

The woman in question entered the room with her own food and sat down. "I like to be busy," she said, moments before they said grace.

Mabel was exhausted. As much as she'd enjoyed the visit to the gardens, it wore her out. It was likely a combination of the stroll through the greenery and also the fresh air. Apart from that, she wasn't used to traipsing around for so long. It was definitely worth it. Besides, the more she did it, the more used to it she would become.

Earl had run a warm bath for her, and Mabel appreciated his effort. He was the perfect husband, ensuring her every need was met, and looking out for her. She appreciated everything he'd done for her and looked forward to a long marriage. It was a pity he had no true feelings for her, because Mabel was the opposite. She'd had feelings for Earl from early on. She knew it was possible her feelings were more on the side of thankfulness than love, but she was happy, and that was the main thing.

She climbed into the bath and let herself sink into it. Before Earl had diagnosed her pregnancy, Mabel hadn't noticed her belly was growing, but now it was very evident. Soon she would need bigger clothes. They were already a little tight, but bearable.

Grateful for her current situation, Mabel allowed herself to relax into the water, but didn't close her eyes. Not even for a moment. She knew if she did, she would fall asleep. That was not conducive to her safety. Earl had warned her not to fall asleep in the water.

The house was enormous compared to anywhere she'd lived before, except, of course, the orphanage. It was old and run down. This building, her home, was not terribly old. At least she guessed it wasn't. The town of Pleasant Valley was settled around the time she was born, so not that long ago, in the scheme of things.

She'd been sheltered most of her life, and only since she'd married Earl had she learned the way of the world. He was a kind man, her husband. His voice was gentle, and all his dealings with her had been pleasant. When she thought about it, Mabel realized she hadn't been treated kindly for a very long time.

Leaving the orphanage, she had struggled. It seemed like forever before she met Vern, who promised to take care of her. Little did she know what that involved. Still, at the time it was a lifesaver for the bedraggled young girl who had nowhere to live, and little income. Barely enough to feed herself.

Mabel knew now she'd been tricked. Vern had taken her in for his own purposes, and that didn't sit right with Mabel. Her hands went to her belly. "I'll always look after you," she whispered, and prayed she could fulfill her promise.

She startled at the tap on the door. "Mabel? Are you alright in there? It's getting late." Earl was right. She'd been in there for a long time. The water was near cold, and she needed to get out.

"Coming," she called back. It had been a big day, and Mabel was ready for sleep.

Chapter Twelve

Earl couldn't believe how long it had been since Mabel had arrived. Already a month, and her belly had grown immensely in that time.

It was now obvious she was further along in her pregnancy than he'd first thought. Her overall condition when she'd arrived had been appalling. If he hadn't known better, he would think she'd been living on the streets. Except for the way she dressed.

His previously thin and gaunt wife had now filled out nicely. She was far more than skin and bone, and appeared far more healthy. She even had color in her cheeks.

"Good morning," he whispered against her ear. His arms wrapped around her as they lay in bed was how he loved to wake each morning. His hands cupped her belly as he held her protectively. There seemed to be no more threat, as Vern had not appeared. That didn't mean he wouldn't turn up, but it became more unlikely with each passing day.

He leaned forward and kissed his wife's cheek. That was when it happened. "Oh! Did you feel that?" Mabel exclaimed. "What was that?"

Earl chuckled. "That, my dear, was our baby moving. He's letting us know he is alive and doing well." It had taken her awhile, but Mabel had finally gotten used to him calling the baby *their* baby. He'd told her from the start he would be the baby's father. It wasn't the child's fault if its father was a criminal.

If Earl had his way, Vern would disappear and never be heard of again. He prayed it would be so, but didn't hold his breath. He strongly believed if Vern had intended to reclaim Mabel like a discarded package, he would have done so by now.

Mabel turned to face him. "Don't you mean *she's* letting us know?" She smiled then. It was an ongoing joke between them. They would find out in a few months when the baby made its appearance, and not until then.

Delivering Mabel's baby would be difficult. Not from a medical point of view, but because it would be difficult to deliver the baby and also give her the support she needed as his wife.

He rolled over and reached for his glasses. "We'll see," he said, and grinned at her before climbing out of bed. "You stay as long as you want."

Pulling the covers up over her shoulders, Mabel snuggled back underneath and closed her eyes. She never stayed in bed long after Earl was up. They spent as much time together as they could. Today,

Earl had a clinic. Some days, he wished he wasn't a doctor and could stay home with his wife all day.

Then again, whatever his vocation, he would still need to go out to work. He quickly dressed, then headed toward the bathroom.

Staring at his reflection, Earl knew he was a better man because of Mabel. He lathered up his face and lifted the razor. He'd never enjoyed shaving, and some days became lazy. Since his wife's arrival, he'd shaved each and every day.

Since when had he cared if he was clean shaven or not? He knew the answer, and the reason. Earl had begun his married life taking on his brother's responsibilities. It was a completely different story now. He had fallen in love with Mabel, and didn't know what he would do without her.

He only wished she felt the same.

Earl knew from the start theirs would be a loveless marriage. He'd even demanded it was a convenience, rather than a real marriage. As the days and weeks had rolled on, his feelings for Mabel had grown.

He splashed water on his face to remove the remnants of the shaving cream. He dried his face, then rinsed the brush, returning his supplies to the cupboard.

Earl stared at his reflection once more. He looked the same as he did a month ago, but knew he was a completely different person. The man he was today was a far better man than before he met his wife. He wasn't sure if it was simply because she was his brother's betrothed, or whether it was Mabel herself. He felt convinced it was the latter.

There was movement outside the bathroom, and he opened the door. Mabel stood there, looking desperate. It made him laugh that she appeared so desperate to use the facilities. Pregnant women so often need to run to the privy.

He hurried out so she could enter.

"That is so much better," Mabel said as she entered the kitchen. Earl couldn't help but chuckle.

Mrs. Halliwell placed a cup of tea in front of his wife. Since the morning sickness had subsided, she preferred to sit at the table with him while he had breakfast.

"I have a busy clinic today," he said. "I may be a little late for lunch," he told the housekeeper. "Hopefully not, but we'll see."

"Soup is on the menu, so it won't matter," she said. "And freshly baked bread." She buttered two slices of toast and handed them to Earl. They would go nicely with his sausages and eggs. Mabel preferred to wait until he'd left to eat her own meal. She said her stomach felt more settled then. It made no difference to him.

Mrs. Halliwell sat down with them, bringing a cup of tea for herself. "I think it's time," she told Mabel. "I'll arrange for the seamstress to make you some maternity gowns."

Earl agreed. He'd noticed her clothes becoming tighter as the weeks went on and had intended to mention it to Mrs. Halliwell. She was a wealth of knowledge and always knew what to do. He finished up his breakfast and drank down the last of his coffee. "I'll freshen up, then bid you farewell," he said, then kissed his wife on the cheek. Her smile faded at his words. Warmth filled Earl to know she would miss him. Was it really only a little over a month since she'd arrived? He felt as though he knew her thoroughly, but always wanted to learn more.

He strode into the bathroom and freshened up, then headed toward the clinic. As he unlocked the door, Earl noticed the long line of patients. Most had arrived early. He put on a brave front and smiled as he ushered them into the waiting area. "Good morning, everyone," he said, far more cheerfully than he felt.

He picked up his patient list for the day and called his first patient. "Mrs. Harcourt," he said, ushering her into his surgery. "What can I do for you today?"

Earl inwardly sighed as he listened to her non-existent ailment. He tried to remember this patient was paying him to listen. He sat a little straighter and hoped the next patient came with something a little more exciting.

"Tell me about your day," Mabel said as they crossed the road and strolled toward the church garden.

They'd begun bringing a snack along, as Mrs. Halliwell worried, particularly for Mabel, that she didn't eat enough in the afternoon. As they sat on the wooden bench surrounded by the fragrant plants Mabel loved so much, Earl unwrapped their afternoon delicacies. He chuckled when his wife leaned across to see what they had today.

"Carrot cake," Earl said, handing her a slice. "Good for both you and the baby." He took a mouthful and ate slowly. He wanted to savor every bit. Flavor burst in his mouth, and he reached for another slice.

Besides, he didn't want to share how boring his day had been.

"Not only is Mrs. Halliwell an excellent cook, but she cares about both of us." Mabel's words rang true to him. He had inherited the housekeeper from the previous doctor, and at first had fought against a housekeeper. Particularly, a live-in housekeeper.

Soon it was clear she was an important member of his household. Someone he truly couldn't do without. The woman was indispensable, but over the years, had become more like a family member than an employee.

It seemed he'd distracted her enough to get away with not telling her about his day.

She finished her cake and turned to study him. "I suppose that means your day wasn't good?"

He scowled. "You know I can't breach the privacy of my patients, but it was very… shall we say, mundane?"

She raised her eyebrows. "At least it wasn't horrific. No broken bones or half amputated legs, then?" Mabel laughed then, and he couldn't help but join her. What was it about his wife that lightened his mood and set his heart racing?

He leaned across and pulled her toward him, wrapping Mabel in his arms. He kissed her forehead, then moved to her lips. "Mabel Carpenter, do you know how much I love you?" The words were out before he even thought about them.

Mabel stiffened under his touch. She turned to stare into his face, and her tears swam in her eyes. "I love you too," she whispered. "I had no idea you felt the same." She leaned in and rested her head against his chest, and Earl didn't want to be anywhere else. Right here with Mabel was where he wanted to be.

She suddenly sat up and reached for his hand. "Feel that," she said, almost giggling. "Baby is dancing."

Earl couldn't help but feel her joy. In a few short months, they would get to meet their baby. He rejoiced in the fact he was able to bring his wife back to full health and ensure their child was in the best health he could be. Earl stared at her belly, then turned to Mabel. He couldn't help but grin. "That's a sign of a healthy babe," he told her, and Mabel snuggled into him again.

They sat on the wooden bench, lapping up the sun. They were shaded where they sat, but still caught a little afternoon sun. Earl pulled out his pocket-watch after it seemed they'd been there for at least an hour. The fresh air each day was doing his wife good, and he encouraged it.

He stood, then helped Mabel to her feet. She pouted.

It was the same every day when they headed for home. She'd found her special place, and he hated to drag her away, but supper awaited.

As always, Mabel took her time strolling down the pathway to return home. They crossed the road and turned the corner. At the edge of the road, she stopped sharply, almost pulling him over. Earl glanced about. People shuffled along the boardwalk, but he saw nothing that raised alarm bells.

He knew there had to be a good reason she'd stopped so abruptly. He turned to Mabel—she was deathly white.

"No!" Mabel whispered, then slapped her hands to her mouth. Turning to Earl, she grabbed his hand and dragged him in the opposite direction, and back to the gardens. When they were out of sight, she told him, "It's Vern. We have to hide, can't have him see us," she panted, trying to speak while running, and having difficulty breathing.

Earl hadn't seen anyone. Not a soul, so wasn't sure what she'd seen. Besides, if Vern was coming for her, he would have done it a very long time ago. Wouldn't he?

Suddenly there was a disturbance behind them, footsteps that got quicker and quicker. And closer.

It was then he knew Mabel was right—Vern was here in Pleasant Valley. He had to get her away from him.

Chapter Thirteen

Mabel's heart was pounding.

By the time they reached the very back of the gardens, she was breathless and lightheaded. She willed herself not to faint.

The area was hidden from the street, and she hoped it meant Vern wouldn't see them. It was far more dense with trees here. It was originally on the edge of the forest, but had since been transformed into part of the church gardens.

It was a peaceful place, these gardens, but today had become a place of terror.

Hidden behind a number of trees was a wooden bench. She'd learned many of the parishioners used this area for contemplation. It was peaceful here, and if it wasn't for the circumstances they found themselves in, Mabel would surely enjoy being here.

Earl sat her down, then crouched down in front of her. "Take a deep breath and let it out slowly," he whispered.

They knew these gardens better than most and knew where they could go and not be found. At least she prayed that would be the case.

Earl's fingers were around Mabel's wrist, no doubt checking her pulse. "You need to slow your heart rate, otherwise you'll pass out."

She already knew that, and didn't need to be told. Mabel immediately bit her lip. She was glad she hadn't said the words out loud—Earl was trying to help, but she felt like snapping at him. And she knew the reason.

Vern was in town.

Surely the sheriff had been tracking him? Except Mabel knew it wasn't true. Other lawmen had endeavored to locate Vern and had been unsuccessful. All that despite her telling the sheriff exactly where to find him. She knew the reason— they were too slow in taking action.

Knowing Mabel was a witness to his atrocities, Vern wouldn't stay put, she was certain. He might be a criminal and a murderer, but he wasn't a fool. She always knew he would spend his days looking for her, to eliminate the threat to his freedom.

"That's a little better," Earl said, still holding her wrist. "Are you certain it was Vern? I thought he would be long gone by now." His eyes pierced her, and it was all Mabel could do not to squirm under his gaze.

"It's him," she whispered. "I'll never forget him." Earl frowned. Had he taken her words the wrong way? "When I watched him murdered that man, the vision was etched in my memory forever." Earl let go of her wrist and instead clamped his hands over hers. The action meant everything to Mabel.

The sound of leaves crunching had her on high alert. Had Vern found them? She gasped, but was relieved to see it was Preacher Jones. "Is everything alright out here?" he asked, his gaze taking in the scene in front of him.

Mabel shook her head, and the preacher appeared puzzled. She tried to explain, but she spoke so quickly, her words only came out garbled.

"What we need," Earl said, squeezing her hand, "is for you to fetch the sheriff. Go straight to the sheriff's office, tell him where we are, and simply say *Vern is in town.*"

The preacher frowned. "Vern is in town? Sheriff Charleston will understand that message?"

"He will. Please hurry. And please, be careful." Earl slid onto the seat next to Mabel as the preacher hurried away. Mabel could see the concern on his face, and knew she must appear anxious as well. Vern was not someone to be messed with.

It seemed like forever before the sheriff arrived, along with the deputy, but it allayed some of her fears. "You're certain he's here?" the sheriff asked before he spoke another word. He sounded skeptical. Even his expression proved that.

"I know what I saw," Mabel said firmly. "I don't know how he found me, but he did. Now you need to arrest him." She glared at the sheriff. After all this time, she thought the man knew what he was doing. Apparently not.

The moment he set eyes on her, Vern would know she was carrying his baby. If he wasn't behind bars, he would claim the baby as his own. Mabel wasn't prepared to hand her baby over to such a dreadful man. She would die before she allowed it to happen. "He can't have my baby," she whispered, emotion overcoming her.

Earl pulled her close. "No, he can't," he said, trying to soothe her.

"He'll be hanged before that can happen," the sheriff said.

"There you are!" Vern's voice rang out across the previously peaceful gardens.

The sheriff's head shot up, and he turned to face Vern.

The deputy's hand was on his gun, but they all hoped it wasn't needed.

"Leave me alone," Mabel shouted at him. By this time, both Earl and Mabel were standing, and her swollen belly was in plain sight. Vern stared at it.

Earl pushed her behind him, trying to protect Mabel from the killer. But he wasn't quick enough. "That my baby in your belly?" His gaze pierced her, and Mabel was dumbstruck. For once, she didn't know what to say.

Vern stood silent for long moments, as though mesmerized by the thought he was going to be a father. He would be the worst kind of role model for any child, and there was no way Mabel would hand her child over to Vern.

"It's my baby," Earl said clearly. "Mabel is my wife."

Vern studied him for what seemed like an hour, but was probably only seconds. "I don't believe you," he shouted.

Mabel was petrified. To get to her and his baby, he would kill anyone who got in his way. Knowing the man he really was, she was convinced it was true. Tears ran down her face and she wiped at them, knowing her tears wouldn't change a thing.

"You can believe what you want," Earl said, taunting him with every word. "Mabel and I are having a baby together. It has nothing to do with you." She felt Earl stiffen, then he reached back and pushed her further behind him. "Keep out of sight," he whispered.

She couldn't let Earl sacrifice himself for her. Her decision made, Mabel stepped out from behind her husband. Staring at Vern, she let him know how much she despised him. "You are not human," she said. "You're a monster. I will not allow you to take my baby."

Vern stood silently for about thirty seconds, then, as if in slow motion, reached under his jacket. Her heart pounded and this time she was certain she would faint. Pulling out a gun, he lifted his hand and pointed it at Mabel. She always knew he would kill her before he'd allow her freedom. But never did she think he would murder his own child.

Mabel screamed, and Earl stepped in front of her. Vern was going to kill her husband, the man she loved with all her heart.

"Please, Vern, no!"

A gun shot rang out, the sound piercing her ears. Then the world went black.

When Mabel opened her eyes, Preacher Jones was standing over her. Vern had killed Earl, and her heart was shattered. She would never come back from this. Vern would claim her for his own again, and her baby would be raised by a killer.

"He'll live." Mabel couldn't believe what she was hearing. She must be dreaming because that sounded like Earl's voice.

"That's a pity," Sheriff Charleston said, disdain clear in his voice. "Two of us shot at him, and neither finished the job." He almost snarled the words.

Mabel lifted her head and thought she saw Earl.

"Earl? Is that you?" Her voice broke as she spoke. "I thought… I thought you were dead."

He stopped what he was doing and went to his wife's side. "Both the sheriff and deputy shot Vern. Otherwise, he was going to shoot me. Why would you do that with the law standing right there?" He shook his head in disbelief.

"Because he's a dang fool," the sheriff said as he chuckled. "This dang fool will hang, I have no doubt. For now, he will be behind bars. The judge should be here next week, and the world will be rid of the likes of him." Amos leaned down and cuffed Vern despite his injuries. "It's a shame I missed his heart and hit his shoulder instead."

"A great pity," Earl said with meaning.

Her husband was not a cruel man, but Mabel knew he wanted to rid them both of such a vile person. Even if they could only prove one murder by Vern, it was enough for him to hang, according to the sheriff. "Get up," he demanded, kicking Vern in the ribs, then marched him to the jail.

The moment they were out of sight, Earl helped Mabel to her feet and took her in his arms. She rested her head against his chest and reveled in his closeness. Mabel thought she had lost him, and it was the absolute worst moment of her life. She didn't know what she would have done if he had been killed.

Earl filled her heart with joy and her life with love. In some ways, he seemed almost unapproachable when they first married, but cared for her from the moment they met. Despite the circumstances under which they got together, Earl had always looked out for her.

Today was no different. If it hadn't been for the sheriff's fast thinking, and straight shooting by both him and his deputy, neither Earl nor Mabel would be standing here now. Earl's strong arms wrapped around her, Mabel said a silent prayer of thanks. The Good Lord obviously hadn't finished with them yet.

Earl gently pushed her away. "We should get back home. Mrs. Halliwell will wonder where we are."

Mabel agreed. "If she knew what happened, she'd be terrified. Oh, I hope she didn't hear the gunshot." She slapped her hands to her mouth. "The poor thing would be petrified. Oh Earl," she almost cried, "we need to get home and make sure she is alright."

Earl's hand on her back soothed her. "She wouldn't hear it from here. Especially if she was inside the house, as I'm sure she would be. Knowing Mrs. Halliwell, she would be cozy in her kitchen, finishing supper."

He was right, Mabel knew he was. Earl was always the voice of reason, and she appreciated it. What she would have done if he hadn't been there with her at the gardens, Mabel didn't know. She would probably be lying dead on the ground by now.

Her hands flew to her belly. As if trying to tell her she was alright, the baby kicked against her hand. Her heart pounded. Was it really over? Could she and Earl live a long and happy life without worrying about Vern turning up to kill them?

As if she'd said the words out loud, Earl lifted her chin and studied her. "It's over. No more worrying about Vern. He is bound for the hangman's noose." She slumped against her wonderful husband, happy in the knowledge what he said was true.

Epilogue

Three years later...

"Again, Mama?" two-year-old Joshua asked when Mabel closed the book they'd been reading.

"Select another, Joshua, and we'll read that instead." She smiled, and her son ran to the bookshelf. He carefully returned his favorite story, then selected another. He was following in his father's footsteps, and was already studious at such a young age.

Earl was a wonderful father to their son. Except for the housekeeper, no one knew he was not Earl's biological son. They would never tell the boy what terrible person gave him life. What would be the point?

Mabel rubbed her belly. This baby was having a good time dancing today. It was almost non-stop. She was exhausted from all the activity it was going through, and she wanted to lie down and have a nap.

"Papa!" Joshua ran across the room to his father. Earl picked the boy up and hugged him. Joshua wrapped his arms around Earl's neck and rested his head on his father's shoulder. "Book," Joshua said, shoving the newest choice toward Earl.

His father snatched up the book and put the boy to the floor. He glanced across at Mabel and she smiled.

His smile quickly faded. "Everything alright?" he asked, concern etched on his face.

"I'm not sure," Mabel told him, and rubbed a hand across her belly.

As if on cue, Mrs. Halliwell walked into the room with a tray. She glanced at Earl, then Mabel, and walked out of the room again. She returned in record time. "What do you have there, young Joshua?" she asked, as if nothing was amiss. She sat down and the child climbed onto her lap as if he'd done it a thousand times before. Mrs. Halliwell was like a grandmother to Joshua, but didn't often sit long enough to read the boy a book.

"Once upon a time," she began, and a grin spread over his face.

Earl led Mabel into his surgery. "Up on the table with you," he said sternly. She knew he was annoyed she hadn't told him. He had a busy day, and she didn't want to bother him. It was probably nothing. He held her hand and helped her up, then ran his hands across her belly. Earl pulled out his stethoscope and listened.

"How long have you been in labor?" he asked, his frustration clear.

She glanced up at him, trying to hide *her* annoyance. "It began around two." Mabel stared at him then, daring him to become emotional.

Instead, he looked her in the eye. "Two this morning or this afternoon?

Mabel glanced at him. "This morning," she said quietly.

"And it's now what?" he pulled out his pocket-watch. "Five—in the evening?" He gave a low growl then. "Let's get you ready to birth this baby, shall we?"

Her heart fluttered. Even when he was clearly frustrated with her, Earl still ensured she was safe and was properly cared for.

Less than an hour later, Earl delivered his daughter. She had his eyes and his gentle face. As he had done when he'd delivered Joshua, his face lit up when he held his daughter in his hands. He walked over to Mabel, placing the baby in her arms. "Can we call her Isabella? After my mother?" she asked, but already knew Earl wouldn't deny her.

He leaned forward and kissed her forehead. "She's beautiful. Isabella is a beautiful name. I still have work to do here," he said, then returned to finish what he'd started.

It wasn't long before he'd finished playing the doctor and became the proud new father. The moment he had his wife settled, he fetched Joshua to come and meet his little sister. Mabel could see him as the big brother in years to come. He would look after Isabella and take care of her, ensuring she came to no harm.

Mabel couldn't believe how much her life had changed in a little under four years. She always knew God had a plan for her, but had no idea everything would change the day she met Earl at the train station when she arrived to marry his brother.

From the Author

Thank you so much for reading my book – I hope you enjoyed it.

I would greatly appreciate you leaving a review where you purchased, even if it is only a one-liner. It helps to have my books more visible!

~*~

About the Author

Multi-published, award-winning and bestselling author Cheryl Wright, former secretary, debt collector, account manager, writing coach, and shopping tour hostess, loves reading.

She writes both historical and contemporary western romance, as well as romantic suspense.

She lives in Melbourne, Australia, and is married with two adult children and has six grandchildren. When she's not writing, she can be found in her craft room making greeting cards.

Links

Website: *http://www.cheryl-wright.com/*

Facebook Reader Group:
https://www.facebook.com/groups/cherylwrightauthor/

Join My Newsletter:

https://cheryl-wright.com/newsletter/

(and receive a free book)